Even the Dogs

Even the Dogs

Jon McGregor

W F HOWES LTD

This large print edition published in 2010 by
W F Howes Ltd
Unit 4, Rearsby Business Park, Gaddesby Lane,
Rearsby, Leicester LE7 4YH

1 3 5 7 9 10 8 6 4 2

First published in the United Kingdom in 2010
by Bloomsbury

A CIP catalogue record for this book is available
from the British Library

ISBN 978 1 40745 792 5

Typeset by Palimpsest Book Production Limited,
Falkirk, Stirlingshire
Printed and bound in Great Britain
by MPG Books Ltd, Bodmin, Cornwall

FSC
Mixed Sources
Product group from well-managed
forests, controlled sources and
recycled wood or fiber
SA-COC-1565
www.fsc.org
© 1996 Forest Stewardship Council

to Alice

Cut off from hope, we live on in desire.

– Dante Alighieri, *The Inferno*

CHAPTER 1

They break down the door at the end of December and carry the body away.

The air is cold and vice-like, the sky a scouring steel-eyed blue, the trees bleached bone-white in the frosted light of the sun. We stand in a huddle by the bolted door.

The street looks quiet, from here. Steam billows and sighs from a central-heating flue. A television flickers in a room next door. Someone hammers at a fencing post on the far side of the playing fields behind the flats.

An overflow pipe with a fat lip of melting ice drips on to the walkway from three floors up, the water pooling and freezing in the shade of a low brick wall.

Cars drive past, from time to time, their windows fogged and their engines straining against the cold.

We see someone getting out of a taxi parked further up the hill. She leaves the door open, and we see two carrier bags stuffed full of clothes and books and make-up on the back seat. She comes up the short flight of steps, and bangs on the door. This is Laura. She shouts through the letterbox. She gestures for the taxi-driver to wait, and goes round to the side of the building. We see her climbing on to a garage roof and in through the kitchen window of the flat. She stands in the kitchen for a few moments. She looks like she's talking to someone. She climbs out again, drops down from the garage roof, and gets back into the taxi.

Later, in the evening of the same day or the day after that, with the other flats glowing yellow and blue from behind thin curtains and pinned-up sheets, we see Mike scrambling up on to the garage roof. We hear shouting, and something being broken. We see Ben, running down the hill towards town.

We see Heather, another morning, hauling herself up the steps and banging on the door, an opened can in one hand. She shouts through the letterbox and looks through the glass. The old woman from the flat next door comes out and says something. They argue, and Heather bangs on the door again before walking off down the hill towards town.

We see Mike, talking on his phone, his long coat flapping around his knees as he strides out into the road.

The streetlamps come on, slowly, glowing red and then orange and then flickering out again as the dawn unfurls. Frost forms across the playing fields and the grass verges, and is smudged by footprints and tyres and the weak light of the distant sun. Time seems to pass.

★   ★   ★

2

We see Danny, running across the playing fields with Einstein limping along behind him. We peer round the corner of the flats and see him climbing on to the roof of the garages. Einstein looks up, barking and scrabbling at the garage door, and we hear the creak of a window being opened.

The old man in the wheelchair appears. We know him but we don't know his name. He's not even that old but it's something to call him. He inches along the pavement, gripping the wheels with hands wrapped in rags and unravelling gloves, his face twisting with the effort of each small push. Grunting faintly as he goes. Huh. Hah. Huh. He glances towards us but he doesn't stop. Huh. Hah. Huh.

The window opens again, and we see Danny jumping from the roof of the garages, falling, landing awkwardly and stumbling when he tries to get up. He picks up his bag and his blankets and he hurries away down the road towards town, passing the old man in the wheelchair and calling Einstein to follow him, his blankets slung over his shoulder and trailing along the ground and he doesn't look behind him as he goes.

It gets dark, and light, and dark again, and we wonder whether anyone else will come. There are more of us now, and we stand in silence by the door, looking up and down the road.

There's no siren when the police finally arrive. They drive slowly up the hill, peering out from

3

the window at the numbered street signs. They pull over at the bottom of the steps and sit there for a few moments with the engine running, talking on their radios.

Someone looks out of a window on the second floor and turns away, pulling the curtains closed.

The front door of the next flat along opens slightly.

The two policemen get out of the car, rubbing their gloved hands together, squinting against the cold and the low late-afternoon sun. One of them, a young-looking man with pale blue eyes and a thin nose, goes to the boot and takes out a pair of long torches. They walk carefully up to the flat, avoiding the ice creeping down the steps, and we move away from the door. Their breath clouds around their faces and trails off into the air.

The door of the next flat opens further, and an old woman appears. She watches the two men shine their torches through the glass panels of the front door and shout through the letterbox. She's wearing a checked dressing gown, and a pair of slippers in the shape of tiger's paws. She says something to them, folding her arms. The younger policeman turns to her and nods, and when she says something more they ignore her.

A car slows as it passes, stopping for a moment and then driving on.

What took them so long. Where were they.

★   ★   ★

They test the door with their shoulders, and then the younger policeman steps back and kicks at the lock. The door falls open. They both move forward, and turn away again, covering their noses and mouths. They look at each other, and lift their torches to shine a narrow light into the flat's dark hall. The old woman shuffles closer, hugging her arms a little tighter around her chest, and we look past her into the torchlit gloom. The place is a mess, but we knew that already. The walls are scribbled-over and stained, bare wires hanging from the rotten plaster. The floor is covered with bottles and cans and blankets and clothes, a pile of car tyres, shards of glass. And there must be a foul smell, the two men's hands still pressed over their noses and mouths and their faces still half turned away. The younger man coughs, as though something is sticking in the back of his throat. The older man puts a hand to his colleague's arm, speaking quietly.

They don't see us, as we crowd and push around them. Of course they don't. How could they. But we're used to that. We've been used to that for a long time, even before. Before this. Their boots crunch and snap on the debris-covered floor. They walk slowly, and they let the light of their torches lead the way. They call out, something like Hello, police, hello. They glance at each other, and they move further into the flat.

★　　★　　★

5

The younger man, turning right at the end of the hall where his colleague has turned left, finds the body lying on the sitting room floor. He looks for no more than a second or two, his eyes widening, and then he calls out, backing away, clamping his fist over his mouth. The older man comes through from the kitchen, his feet grinding across more broken glass as he steps past into the sitting room and sees what's there. He flinches slightly, and nods. He shines a torch over the body, the damp clothes, the broken and blistered flesh. He points out something that looks like blood, puddled across the lino, a trail of it leading into the kitchen. The younger man, still standing in the doorway, speaks into his radio, asking for something. They don't speak. They wait. They look at the body. We all crowd into the room and look at the body. The swollen and softening skin, the sunken gaze, the oily pool of fluids spreading across the floor. The twitch and crawl of newly hatched life, feeding.

It's Robert. But we knew that already.

The sky is darkening outside, a faint red smudge along the treeline by the river, the clouds stretching low and thin towards the ground.

The older policeman tugs at his shirt collar, pulling his tie away from his neck, muttering something to his colleague as he pushes past, leading the way down the cluttered hallway and out into the cold clean air.

Outside, the woman with the tiger-paw slippers and the checked dressing gown is waiting. She asks something, and they hold up their hands and shake their heads. The older man fetches a roll of blue and white tape from the car and cordons off the area around the door. The woman watches them, chewing the inside of her lip. Her skin is dry and loose on her face, gathered in small folds around her jaw. She talks to the younger policeman for a few moments, shaking her head, peering past him towards the open door. She turns, and shuffles back to her flat.

The two men stand in front of the cordon. A fluorescent light on the wall above them buzzes faintly as it warms up. Lights flicker on along the walkway, a few at a time. The sky darkens to a bruised purple. The men stamp their feet and rub their hands to keep away the cold, and they talk. We look up and down the street, and Danny tells us what it was like when he found him, when he climbed in through the window at the back of the flat and found Robert laid out on the floor.

Penny standing in the doorway, shivering and looking up while Danny climbed in through the kitchen window and jumped down on the floor. Didn't see her at first, and when he did he couldn't understand why she weren't yapping like usual, why she was standing so still. Just like trembling and that. Knew something was wrong straight off, it was too quiet. Never been quiet like that before.

Always been Penny and the other dogs barking and music playing and people shouting to make themselves heard. Penny didn't even turn when he went past. Didn't have the strength. Bag of bones. Just stood there and Danny come rushing back out the room and puked on the floor before climbing straight out the window and he didn't look back.

Three more vehicles pull up outside the flat. This is later. The woman with the tiger-paw slippers has brought the men two mugs of tea, asked questions they decline to answer, and taken the empty mugs away. A group of children have gathered by the flat, trying to see past the policemen and into the hallway, trying to duck under the cordon. But they're gone now, and it's quiet. A man and a woman get out of the first vehicle and carry cases of equipment up the steps, talking to the policemen while they climb into rustling white overalls and pull on clear plastic gloves. A woman in jeans and a long grey coat comes up the steps, carrying a small leather bag. Two men take lights and tripods from the back of another van and stack them at the top of the steps. They all take a pair of plastic foot-covers from a box, balancing on one leg and then the other to slip the elasticated cuffs over their shoes while the younger policeman writes their names in a logbook, their breaths steaming above them and yellowing in the fluorescent light.

The woman with the small leather bag goes into the flat, through the hall and into the room where Robert's body lies. She crouches beside him, touching his cold skin, noting the sunken eyes and swollen lips, the insects, the weeping blisters up and down his body. She nods, checking her watch and writing something in a hardback notebook or diary, telling the policeman what time to write in his notes as she leaves, ducking under the cordon, peeling off her gloves and walking quickly down the steps to her car. She puts her bag down on the passenger seat and turns on the radio. She looks at her mobile phone, a blue glow shining on her face, and then she puts it back in her bag and drives away.

The men with the lights go inside and set them up against the walls, keeping well away from the body, connecting the battery packs and the clamps, and suddenly the room is huge with light, with a bright white light which erupts out of each corner and fixes every wriggling detail into place. The man and woman in white overalls come into the room, joined by another man with a thick tangle of dark hair who looks like he might be in charge. The first man takes photographs while the woman looks carefully over the body, pulling Robert's clothes away from his neck, combing her gloved fingers through his hair and picking through the mess on the floor. She shows the photographer the dark bloodstains trailing across

9

the lino. The younger policeman stands in the hallway, watching, and the man with the dark tangled hair asks him questions. He shakes his head, gesturing towards the front door, smiling briefly at some comment made by the photographer, and for a moment the room feels crowded again, crowded like it was the last time we were all here together with Robert stretched out on the floor the way he always was by the end of the night, with that look on his face he only ever got when he was sleeping. And there he is, snoring, spluttering, reaching out a hand behind his head like he's looking for something to hold on to. One of us, Heather probably, leaning forward to pull his coat more snugly across his broad chest, his shoulders, tucking his hat back on to his head until she sees the rest of us watching. The rest of us sleeping. Danny and Ben and Laura and Mike and Ant and whoever else happened to be around. Or not quite sleeping but closing our eyes and listening to the music coming from the taped-up stereo in the kitchen, some broken-beated lullaby holding us up against the walls and against each other, while our hands fall open and spill the spoons and pipes and empty cans, the scraps of foil and paper and cotton wool. Our crumbs of comfort scattering across the floor. Our open hands.

A phone rings, and the policeman standing by the door pulls it from his pocket, gesturing to the others before ducking out of the room to speak, out through the ruined hallway and the battered front door, and as the door closes behind him we see Robert, and Yvonne, working back to back as they take down the old wallpaper, peeling and picking at it with a paint-scraper and a knife, small curls and flakes falling to the floor like confetti. Sitting by the open front door to eat ham and tomato sandwiches and watch children run up and down the steps. Hanging the new paper over the torn remains of the old, measuring and cutting and pasting, the afternoon passing away while they talk or don't talk or sing along with the radio, and by teatime the last corner of paper is finally smoothed into place, the aching in their arms and their necks rushing up on them both as they stand back to look at their work, their hands sticky with wallpaper paste and sweat.

We never met Yvonne but we see her now. We see things differently now. We see them clearing away the traces of whoever had lived there before, painting and papering over the cracks. Throwing out the things left behind, the stacked magazines and hoarded tins, the rusted mousetraps in the cupboard under the sink. The simple acts of two people making a home together. Bringing new furniture in through the narrow doorway: a bed, an armchair, a sofa, a chest of drawers. Adjusting to each other's presence, each other's movements in the small spaces of their lives. The way he paces and stretches, the way she curls into the chair, the sound of their footsteps, the particular smells of

11

their bodies mingling and filling the air. And now she asks him something, rubbing strings of drying paste from her hands and blowing the hair from her eyes. He looks up, smiling, as she pushes the door closed behind her, as she pulls her t-shirt over her head and unclips her bra. They kiss quickly, pressing together, fumbling for buttons and zips, and we back away into the sitting room, with its freshly painted walls and its picture window looking out over the playing fields, the newly planted trees, the river beyond. We can hear the two of them gasping and whispering against the rattling front door. We can see into the main bedroom, and we can see the double bed squeezed up against the wardrobe, the two sleeping bags zipped together on the bare mattress, the over-spilling ashtray and the clothes piled up everywhere, and when we turn back into the sitting room we see the photographer laying metre-sticks out beside the body on the floor. Taking more notes, and asking questions of the policeman who's come back in from outside. One of the men with the lights notices Penny, finally, her head wedged between her front paws and her ears folded flat against her neck. Her small brown body cold and stiff. The older policeman says something from the front doorway, and they follow his directions into the kitchen as Robert comes back from the street with a pile of steaming chips doused in vinegar which he and Yvonne eat straight from the wrapping, wiping their sticky hands on their clothes before finishing the clearing up and undressing again and squeezing into an over-flowing bath where they soap each other's tired bodies and their genes collide inside her.

They sit there, in the bath, the mirror clouding over with steam and the tap dripping quietly into the still water, and we watch the new wallpaper begin to fade. Sunlight comes in through the kitchen window and the open kitchen door, falls against the striped pattern at the far end of the hall, and bleaches the colour away. The front door blows open, and exhaust fumes from the road drift in and brush against the walls, leaving fine layers of dirt stuck to the traces of grease left by trailing hands.

They top up the bath water, the plunging gush of it suddenly loud in the small hushed room. They're quiet now, warm-blooded and sleepy, the spring air drifting in through the open window and bringing with it the sounds of children being called home for bed, and music, and the faint shouts of football games on the playing fields. He dangles his feet over the end of the bath, and she leans her head against his ankles, and they both close their eyes.

The steam from the bath curls out into the hallway, easing the wallpaper away from the wall. Peppered spores of mould thicken and spread towards the ceiling. Rainwater seeps through the worn pointing on the front of the building and pushes through the plaster, the damp spreading outwards like an old bruise. The varnish on the doorframe cracks as the timber swells and softens and gradually rots away.

Later, when the water has cooled again, she stands up, awkwardly, the water streaming down her changed body and splashing into the bath. Her breasts are rounder now, heavier, and her stomach is swollen, her skin stretched taut. She grabs the edge of the sink as she climbs out, and presses a hand against the painful curve of her spine. He takes a towel from the hook on the door and wraps it round her body, holding out his arm to support her weight while she carefully pats herself dry.

Crayon scribbles appear, low on the wallpaper by the heaps of shoes and boxes of toys. Dated felt-tip stripes creep up the wall by the doorframe, tracking their daughter's growth a thumb's width at a time. Tiny shoes nudge in amongst the adult-sized ones, and bigger shoes take their place. Tea-stains the colour of old photographs splash across the wall, lingering long after the broken cups are cleared away. A dent the size of a fist or a fore-head is hidden by a framed school portrait. The damp patches spread further, and the paper sags away from the wall, and the ceiling stains a dark-ening nicotine yellow. The door is kicked from its hinges, and rehung. More framed pictures are put up on the wall.

They scoop their daughter from the bath. This is

14

Laura, we realise. They carry her from the room in the snug white wrap of a towel, chatting happily and playing with her mother's hair. He leans down and kisses her damp forehead, breathing in the soapy smell of her, and he watches as his wife carries her into the small bedroom and puts her to bed, and he fetches a bottle of whisky from beneath the kitchen sink.

In the bathroom, dark lines of mould creep along the grouting between the tiles, and the tiles crack and fall away from the wall. The sink is pulled from its fixings and breaks in two, the cracked pipes spilling water across the floor until they're capped and disconnected. The toilet stops flushing, blocks, and overflows, and the sludgy water pools in the corner of the room where the floor slopes down a little. The mirror above the sink is smashed into pieces.

In the kitchen, the man and woman in white overalls shine their torches around the room and push at the window. It swings open, creaking against the frame. They lean forward, seeing how large the gap is, looking out at the garage roof below. They look at the bloodstains in the sink, and take samples. They write things down in their notebooks, they take photographs, they shine their torches carefully across the surface of the worktop and the floor.

When they come back into the sitting room there are two more of them, wearing black suits and black shoes sheathed in plastic foot-covers. They tape plastic bags over Robert's hands and head, wrap his whole body in a plastic sheet, and squeeze him into a thick white plastic bag. It takes four of them to get him into the bag, and one of them seems to make a joke about it. They seal the zip with a numbered lock. They lift him on to a stretcher, awkwardly, and it takes six of them to carry him out to the waiting van.

The photographer stays behind and takes pictures of the room without him in it. The empty space on the floor, which seems enormous now. The marks and stains around where he lay. His hat, which must have slipped from his head when he fell.

The two men who set up the lights stand in the hallway, talking quietly, waiting for the photographer to finish. He nods at them as he leaves, and they turn off the lights, the older policeman shining his torch while they pack the equipment away. The hot bulbs glow faintly for a few moments, and they carry everything else out to the van while they wait for the last ebb of light to cool.

We stand together in the hallway, uncertainly. We can hear the two policemen talking outside, the crackle and mutter of their radios. We can hear footsteps moving around upstairs, and somebody laughing. We can hear, faintly, Robert and Yvonne in the bath, splashing each other, asking for the soap. But when we look, there's no one there, and the tiles are still cracked, fallen into the empty

16

bath, and the sink has still been pulled from the wall. The hooks on the back of the door have been ripped out. The door to the small bedroom has been kicked from its hinges and propped against the wall. The framed pictures have been taken down, the glass smashed on the floor and the photographs torn into small fluttering pieces, each brighter square of wallpaper cratered by a fist-sized hole. Wine bottles have been broken against the doorframes, bleeding long red stains down the walls. The lino tiles have been studded with cigarette burns, and half of them peeled up off the floor. People have come and gone, and come and stayed, and left their rubbish piled up in the hall. We wait, not looking at one another, not sure what to do next. One or two of us leave, perhaps to go with him. Time seems to pass. We can hear them in the bathroom still, the tap dripping into the water, the low static murmur of their voices.

Outside, it gets lighter, and darker, and as the sky begins to lighten again behind the curtains in Laura's room her mother creeps in and sits on her bed. We watch as she brushes the hair from her sleeping daughter's eyes. Laura wakes up, and frowns. Her mother puts a finger to her lips, reaching under the bed to pull out a bag she packed with clothes and money the night before, and while Laura gets dressed she gathers a few of her books and toys and stuffs those in as well. Laura crouches on the floor to pull on her shoes, and then the two of them slip from the room and out of the flat, closing the front door with an almost inaudible squeeze and click, and then the two of them are gone. The morning's light begins to filter through the thin orange curtains, and the shallow impression of Laura's body on her mattress slowly fades. The scent of her lingers in the hollow fibres of the rumpled pillow, and in the turned-back duvet, and in the vests and pants and t-shirts which spill in bitter fistfuls from her drawers. The book she was being read is left unfinished, broken-backed on the floor. Dust settles. And then the two of them are gone.

He wakes up. Robert, this is. He wakes up, and every day it seems as though they've only just left. He wakes with a jolt, as if at the sound of the softly closing door, and remembers that the two of them are gone. The room is suddenly much darker. We sink to the floor. The view from the window is clouded by an unfamiliar condensation on the glass. The heat from the lights and the voices and the bodies of the men and women who have been in the room takes a few hours to fade. As it does so, and as the whole flat begins to cool, the condensation hardens into thin tracings of ice, and splinters of light from the dawn outside crack slowly into the room.

We get up, and we leave the flat. We're not sure what else we can do. In the street, the men slide

Robert's body into a van with darkened windows, and we all climb in beside him. There isn't enough room, but it seems like the right place to be. In the circumstances. They slam the doors closed. The air inside is hushed and still, the steel floor shining with cold. Two of the men stand outside, talking to the younger policeman and the photographer, and the man with the dark tangled hair. At the top of the steps, the woman with the checked dressing gown is standing with her arms folded, watching, the older policeman beside her. People have appeared on the walkway, and at windows on the upper floors. A group of children are standing on the pavement, pushing each other, shouting questions. The two men, and the younger policeman, climb into the front of the van, and there's a rush of cold damp air before they close the doors. They start the engine, and the tyres slip and squeak as we drive away down the hill. We look back, and we see the garage roof behind the flat, where Danny jumped and slipped and ran off looking for someone to tell. And we see Danny

CHAPTER 2

They carry his body through the city at dusk and take him away to the morgue.

And we see Danny, stumbling away from the garages at the back of the flats, tumbling down the hill like he's about to fall, rubbing at his cheeks with the backs of his hands in great angry gestures which look almost like punches, wiping at the tears which haven't yet fallen from a face still twisted with fear. Einstein beside him, snapping and whining and trying to keep up, held back as always by the weight of her broken

Had to find someone and tell them was all he could think. Had to find Laura and let her know, had to find Mike. But tell her what, him lying on the floor like that, one leg bent wrong under the other and one hand over his mouth like he could smell himself beginning to rot. Tell her what, he died peacefully, they took him in and did everything they could but in the end there weren't nothing to be done. He didn't suffer. Couldn't tell her that. Didn't know much about it but knew it weren't nothing like that. He had all his friends around him when fuck

Through the darkened windows of the van we watch him, slipping and hurrying down the hill to the main road and the underpass and through the darkened windows we see the city passing us by, whole streets abandoned to the cold, faint shadows moving behind curtains backlit by a flickering pale blue. Christmas decorations dip and swing between telegraph poles and skeletal trees, hang from garage doors, trail from the lids of bins spilling over with crumpled paper and packaging foam. Coloured lights snap on and off in front-room windows, and around shop-front displays, and we follow him down to the bottom of the

Danny, were you the last one to see him?
Fuck should I know.
Was anyone there when you found the body?
Don't know I didn't hang around.
What did you do? Where did you go?
Fucking ran what do you think. What would
  you

He'd been away was what he'd tell the police. He decided. If they came looking for him, if they had a reason to come looking for him, which if he kept his mouth shut why would they. Unless some cunt. He'd been out of town. He'd gone to his brother's house, for Christmas, he'd got the idea into his

21

head that they could have a like a family thing for once. Danny and his brother Tony and Tony's new wife and them two kids which weren't even Tony's. Weren't much of a family. Weren't much of an idea anyhow because Tony kicked him out on Boxing Day, like gave him a cold turkey sandwich and told him to fuck off but that was where he'd been and that was what he'd tell the police. If they showed up, if they took him in and asked him questions like

We've all known people dead but aint many ever seen it. Thought he'd look asleep or something but weren't nothing like that at all. Was more like, what. Flies and maggots and stuff leaking over the floor. And the smell of it. Churns in your guts and comes pouring out your mouth like

Two days to get back from his brother's, two days of walking and hiding in train toilets and jumping over barriers and sleeping in carparks and walking some more and carrying Einstein when her leg got too bad. Big fucking dog to carry but what else could he do. When it was his fault about the leg anyway. And this was the welcome he got, no cunt anywhere and Robert laid out dead and no clue what's going on at all. Had to find Mike was the thing, Mike would sort it, Mike would know what was going on and what to do. But had to find Laura as well, had to tell Laura before some other cunt got there first. Like Ben or some

22

cunt like that. Had to find somewhere to score. And his own brother had shut the door on him, had said

The driver talks to the policeman in the front, and for the first time we can hear what they say. Is this your first one, he's asking, and the policeman says Yes, just about, first proper one like this, and the two men laugh and say You'll soon get used to it, chap, it's a busy time of year. We follow Danny down to the bottom of the hill, trailing his blankets, tripping over the sodden ragged hems of his jeans, turning to call and hurry Einstein along. The van sweeps up the sliproad at the interchange, and we lose sight of him for a moment as he stumbles down into the underpass, the weight of Robert's body shifting in the bag between us as we turn on to the exit road and see Danny climbing the steps back up to the street. We see him shaking his head, taking off his glasses and wiping them clean across his coat, looking around for anyone he knows. But there's no one. Only Einstein, sitting at his feet and panting hard, standing and following as Danny strides away again, the way he always walks, swinging his arms too hard like he's struggling up a steep hill or something, off towards Barford Street and the markets, turning to look at us for a moment as we drive past and leave him behind, as we weave smoothly through empty one-way streets past loading bays and bus shelters and somewhere out beyond, accelerating away up the steep ramp of the flyover towards the bruise-dark clouds of the blackened He saw Sammy, down on the corner of Barford Street and Exchange Street. Saw him from the top of the road but he knew it was him, weren't no one else it could be. That great long beard and the screwed-up eyes and the way he shuffled around like his feet were chained together or something. Called out as soon as he saw him. Sammy, Sammy mate, Sammy, near enough running down towards him in his usual spot on the corner with the benches and bins and flower-pots and that sculpture of fuck knows what. Sammy mate. Sammy. His voice ragged and breathless with the pace he'd kept up since climbing out of the window at the flat. Sammy pissing into a bin, waving fuck off over his shoulder. Sammy, mate, I'm looking for Laura, have you seen her, do you know where she is? Sammy turning and putting his knob away, wiping his hands on his filthy trousers. Staggering with the effort of focusing on Danny, his mouth opening and closing like he'd already forgotten the question. Danny kept moving, kept walking, couldn't stop, looked away up Barford Street and back the way he'd come, headed off up Exchange Street and away towards the Abbey Day Centre. Not seen no cunt for days, Sammy called out, and Danny turned back to listen, walking backwards for a moment to see if there was anything more. Not seen no cunt for days, Sammy said again, almost to himself, sitting down heavily and reaching around on the floor for his bottle while a pigeon circled in from a rooftop, settled on the edge of the bin, and pecked at a sodden kebab. You can fuck off an all, Sammy said when he heard it, spitting in its general direction, the phlegm trickling through his beard as the pigeon flew up over the marketplace, the station, the multi-storey carpark and the office block and the long dwarfed spire of the

It was the wife was the problem. Tony's wife. She had a long memory was the problem. Tony had been all right before. He'd let Danny stop round there sometimes. He'd sorted him out. They went back a long way and they had a what, they had a way of dealing with things. Like an understanding. But then he'd met that woman. Nicola. Nicolah-di-dah. Danny had turned up one time, hadn't been there for months on account of some previous misunderstanding which would have been forgotten by then if it was down to Tony, but now it was different because she was there, Nicola, his new wife, and it was obvious she thought she knew all about him. Grabbed hold of her kids and took them upstairs, didn't even say hello or nothing, left him standing there in the lounge thinking what the fuck have I done this time. Tony said Sorry but she's just kind of nervous and that, with the kids and everything, you know how it is. Nervous was right. The way she swept them off upstairs like that she must have thought he was like what, infectious or something. Like he could pass on all the troubles he had as easy as sneezing. Aint that simple, Nicolah. Aint that simple at all. Takes years of

Had to find someone and tell them. Jesus, what was it, what had happened. Leave town for a week and you come back and he's dead and everyone else vanished like a fuck like a puff of what like a giro cheque. Passed a phonebox on Exchange Street and thought about calling the police from there and telling them about Robert. Found some fag-ends on the floor outside and put them in his tin. Got as far as opening the door before he changed his mind because what was he going to say, what was

Where did you go when you left the scene?
  Ran down the hill, went under the underpass, went into town.
  Why did you run?
  I didn't run but I was like scared and that.
  Scared of what?
  Don't know, I was just scared.
  Where did you go?
  Was looking for someone.
  Where did you

Through the market, down past the Lion and the newsagent's and the bookie's. Straight over the main road and across the roundabout and round the side of the old boarded-up warehouse to the hostel where he'd seen Laura that last time. Buzzed at the door but no one answered. Looked up at the windows but couldn't see no one there. Pints of milk keeping cold on the windowsills, trainers and boots hanging out to air, but the curtains all shut and no sign of anyone awake. Looked in through the office window and saw that what's her name Ruth on the other side of the bars, clicking away on the computer with her face all lit up by the screen. Banged on the window but when she looked up she only pointed back at the door. Fucksake. Buzzed at the door again and some other bloke's voice came out the speaker going Sorry, mate, we're not open yet, usually you'd have to come back at five but we're full tonight, is there anything we can help you with? I'm looking for someone, Danny said, I'm looking for a friend, she's staying here, I need to come in and talk to her. Bloke goes What's her name and when Danny said Laura he didn't say nothing for a minute then he said She's not here. She was here a few days ago, Danny said, where's she gone. Bloke said I can't tell you that I can't help you, mate. Danny said It's fucking cold out here will you let me in so we can have a proper conversation or what, like she must be here, she was going to stay another couple of weeks at least. I need to talk to her. Bloke said I can't help you, mate, sorry, and if that's your dog we don't let dogs in either, and then he didn't say nothing else even though Danny kept buzzing and buzzing and shouting into the speaking grille. Banging on the office window didn't help neither, the glass was all toughened and anyway the bars were there and Ruth didn't even look she just kept clicking away on that fucking computer and what the fuck was she looking at that was so interesting anyway and why wouldn't they tell him where the fuck Laura had

Through the alleyway past the memorial gardens, looking for fag-ends among the rosebushes and cider bottles, round the back of the council offices, checking the parking meters all down past the tyre fitter's and the sofa warehouse and then up the ramp to the wet centre. Which was shut over Christmas and had a sign on the door saying where else the regulars could go for help if they needed it. Only most of them didn't want to go nowhere else and were just sitting it out in the doorway until it opened again. Knew one of them, Bristol John, and asked him if he'd seen Laura or any of the others and he thought about telling him what had happened to Robert. But it was too late in the day to get any sense so he turned and kept going, past the council offices, the housing office, the shops on Exchange Street and the tiny almost hidden doorway of the Abbey Day Centre. Didn't look like no one was there except Maureen and Dave and that bloke who's always in the corner and never says a word except Cheers when they give him a cup of tea. Maureen looked pleased to see him. She always looked pleased to see anyone. Looked like someone's auntie or granny with her cardigans and her white hair and her glasses on a chain around her neck but she never took grief from no one. I'll have none of that from you she said, if anyone tried anything on, and that was usually enough to do the trick. Made Danny a cup of tea without asking, and started on talking about Christmas and New Year and where had everyone got to, her words coming out in one mouthful the way they always did like she was scared that stopping for breath would give someone the chance to turn away. Which they often did. She was all right but she had a lot to say. Danny didn't sit down. He couldn't. He looked in the games room, the laundry room, the toilets, the computer room, and he paced back through the lounge each time to make sure, like maybe this was all some game, some trick they were playing, and they were going to jump out and go ta-dah and all that. But there weren't no one there and no one jumped out and no one said nothing. Maureen said There's been no one in all day, love, there's been no one here since Christmas Day. She said We had a bit of trouble here on Christmas Day mind you, we had a couple of girls overdosing in the toilets, the ambulance men came and sorted them out but still it doesn't look good does it? They should have known we don't have any of that sort of thing here. It gave us all quite a fright, really. So perhaps everyone's just keeping out of the way after that, do you think, Dave? We had the police in asking questions and everything, I mean. Or maybe they've all just gone off to that new winter shelter, maybe they'll be back when that packs in. Maybe the tea's better there, she said, looking down at the tea she'd put on the table for Danny, wondering why he hadn't drunk it yet. Danny taking off his glasses to fiddle with the tape on the broken arm, smearing them clean again and Maureen going Have you not had those seen to yet, love? You want to get them fixed up, they're half falling off your face. Bloke in the corner just watching them both, his eyes half closed, his head wobbling like it was balanced on a plate and being carried aloft through a crowded room and Dave in the kitchen calling out Now then, Mo, no one does better tea than you. But no one there. Not Mike. Not Laura. Not Heather or Ben or Steve or Ant or any of that crowd. Just Maureen waiting for him to drink his cup of tea, and fetching a bowl of biscuits to take out for Einstein without waiting to be asked. Saying if I didn't know better I'd be worried, only it's like this sometimes, some days you can't move for folk and other days you're sitting around wondering what to do with

And if he found Laura what was he going to say. It's about your dad. You'd better sit down. The thing is. And what was he thinking, like she'd be grateful or something, like she'd be pleased he was the one to have told her. Like that was going to make things easier. When she was all mixed up about him anyway, from not seeing or knowing him all those years, from her mum giving her all horror stories that she never knew were true or not. What's it called. Conflicted. Said she hadn't been able to remember what he looked like until she found some photos her mum had kept hidden, and then when she met him he looked all wrong. Told him about living with her nan, and then later just with her mum, and not knowing what to say when kids at school asked about her dad. But, fucksake. She can't have been the only one whose dad weren't around. He told her that, Danny did. One time when they were waiting together for a kid to show up with the gear. She said she'd always kept wondering about him and all that, hoping for a birthday card, thinking one year maybe he'd turn up on Christmas Day for a surprise. Her mum told her she wouldn't let him in the house if he did. But, fucksake. The way she went on about it. One out of two aint bad. Should try living in a children's home and see how fucking conflicted you end up then, he told

Off again past the back of the council offices, Einstein not wanting to leave the food behind but limping along beside him all the same. Past the alleyway down to the back of the shopping centre and through the multi-storey carpark and there still weren't no one there. Could have told Maureen. She would have told the police for him. Out on to the Royal Square. Could have asked to use the phone and done it himself. They'd have to be told. What the fuck was he thinking. Couldn't just leave Robert lying on the floor. Couldn't just wait while someone else climbed in through the window or broke the door down and found him lying there like that. Tripped on the kerb by the taxi rank and fell on his knees, but so what if anyone saw. Einstein nudging at his ear to see if he was all right. Barking at him to get up. Had to tell someone else first, before he told the police, had to find out if anyone else knew, had to get things straight, things were all too fucking fucked up. Getting up again and stumbling past the office block with the indoor waterfall and that security guard who comes out from behind his desk as soon as anyone catches his eye. And if he found Laura what did he think was going to happen. She was going to cry on his shoulder or something. And then what. Kept walking because what else can you do. The underpass at the end of Station Street. Found some more fag-ends there. The steps. The canal towpath. Probably she wouldn't even let him speak to her after last time after what happened the

Mike would know what to do. Danny thought. Mike might know who those two girls were who'd gone over at the Abbey. Wouldn't be Laura though else Maureen would have said. Mike would know. Hard work hanging out with Mike sometimes but at least he generally knew what to do, in a situation, in a situation like this. Except they'd never been in a situation like this. Fuck. Thing to do now before anything else was find Mike, up at the Parkside squats where they'd been sleeping lately and find him there he must be there. But Laura. But needing to score. But Mike might have some would he fuck would he

If he hadn't gone to his brother's. If he hadn't said all that to Laura. If he'd stuck with Mike. Then none of this would have

Bunch of people outside the Catholic church but it weren't going to open for another hour or something and he had to get sorted first. They did a good lunch, but food weren't important now. Wouldn't keep it down anyway the state he was in. Looked to see if there was anyone he knew. Maggie, and Jamesie, and that girl Charmaine with the baby, standing there pushing him backwards and forwards in the buggy to get him back to sleep. Fucksake, when she first turned up on the scene. Weren't long before she got a place in this mother and baby hostel but before that, Jesus. She'd told Laura about it. Left home because her mum was giving her a hard time about the baby, not giving her no help except a mouthful of You're doing it all wrong and then her mum's bloke said

If you don't shut that fucking kid up I'll fucking shut it up for you. Which like she knew what he was capable of with her mum. She told them all this down the Housing, but all they heard her say was I left home, which meant they could give it all I'm sorry, love, you've made yourself intentionally homeless there's very little we can do. Told Laura she spent three days and nights after that just walking around town. Specially at night, she said. Didn't want to sleep nowhere, in case someone took little Ryan, you get me? What would I have done then? Just kept walking and walking until something worked out, getting all blisters and sores, tucking little Ryan into his buggy under blankets and coats and hushing him to sleep and wiping his tears away. Nicking jars of babyfood for him until she got arrested and someone got on her case and got this place in the hostel sorted out. I lost it a bit them nights though, she told Laura, I don't know what I was up to really, I weren't thinking straight or nothing. But you go different when you've got a kid though, know what I mean? Get like you'd do fucking anything for it. Three days and nights she just kept walking, singing like lullabies to little Ryan and walking all night and nobody noticed a thing. Even outside the Catholic church now she was standing a way apart from the others, pushing the buggy backwards and forwards and looking around in all directions, like standing guard or getting ready to

★ ★ ★

34

Climbed across the lockgates under the flyover, the black timbers glassed with ice, the canal water tumbling into the empty lock with a sound like the blood rushing in his ears. A few caravans and trucks parked up under the flyover, some kids burning cables on a bonfire but no one he knew so he climbed back across the canal and called Einstein and carried on along

Mike had told him hadn't he, Mike had said he was better off not going, said there was no way his brother would let him in the house. So if he'd listened. He should have listened. Seemed like Mike was talking bollocks half the time but then he turned out right. Which was why he'd stuck with him. He'd helped out when Danny first showed up in town, when he'd got taxed for asking someone where he could score. Come up afterwards and offered Danny halves on a ten bag in return for a split on Danny's next giro, helped him get the giro sorted and get a new address for it and all the rest. Waited three days while the giro came through and that was enough to set them up as partners, three days of thieving and begging and scoring just enough to keep from getting sick while they waited for the giro to come in. Which all went at once on the dark and the light and they got through it quick before anyone could find them and take it off

Jesus. Could do with some gear now. Would help. Would help him think a bit straight. Got his script from the chemist as soon as he got to town, before he went up to Robert's, but that was hours ago now and it weren't nearly holding him. Yawns coming on already and the rest would follow soon as. Had just enough for a bag from what his brother had given him when he'd slung him out of the house. When he'd said Danny take this I can't have you here no more, not in your state, not with Nicola and the kids and everything, I've given you a chance but she's had enough she's all on edge. You understand don't you, mate. Boxing Day. Nice one. You know how it is, with the kids, but take this and get yourself sorted. And happy fucking Christmas to you an all, brother. There'd been a bit of a scene then, shouting, banging, kids crying in the house and Nicola's little red car getting its windows broken again but only once he'd taken the money. He was proud but he still needed the money. Found somewhere to score before setting off back. Not hard when you know what you're looking for and it don't take long. Scored just enough to hold him while he got to the chemist's, and kept enough money back to sort him out after that. His own brother and he wouldn't let him in the house. And if he had he wouldn't have been the one to find Robert like that. Would have been one of the others and it would be them staggering around town now going mental with the sight of it instead of him. It was always, why was it always

★   ★   ★

Couldn't get his usual man to answer the phone and he'd been trying all day. Cunt was probably still in bed. No one around to ask for another number but if he didn't get sorted soon he was going to start getting sick he was going to

Down the steps by the locks beneath the railway bridge. The water dark and still and rainbow-slicked with oil. The railway arches fenced off to keep them out but he knew a way through. Dark inside, and a stink of piss and shit and soot but no one there. A heap of rotting blankets, a pair of split boots, cans and bottles and scraps of foil and card, an old paperback book ripped apart at the spine. But no one there. Something scratching and moving

Three days before Christmas Danny had last seen everyone. Up at Robert's flat and everything had seemed fine back then. No one had much gear, there hadn't been much gear around for a while, but there was plenty of benzos and jellies going around, plus the scripts. Nothing to get excited about but enough to keep anyone from getting proper sick. Plus some more drinks than usual and

Walked along the towpath looking in at the water, wondering where to score and wondering where to go for a dig when he did. Rolled a fag from the ends he'd found but he knew it wouldn't do much good. A heron standing watch up ahead, shoulders hunched over, looking in at the water. Heaving into the air on its big baggy wings when Danny got too close, Einstein chasing on ahead and Danny thinking about the works in his bag. The note in his sock weren't worth nothing if he couldn't find no one selling. The heron settled on the opposite bank a hundred yards ahead, folding its wings and hunching its shoulders and dipping its ash-white head towards the water as Danny called Einstein back and scrambled away up the

Only one chair in the room and that was Robert's. Everyone else sat on the floor. Leaning up against the wall which meant Robert was always sat at the centre of things with everyone around him. All his things in easy reach. His cans, his papers, his tobacco. Good job because it took him a lot of time and trouble to stand up and someone mostly had to help him. Big man like that. Drank all day and didn't do anything else. Seemed like the deal was if people brought him food and drink they could hang out in his flat, and it seemed like a good enough deal. Brought him plenty of food enough. Never asked Danny no questions the first time Mike took him up there, and that was the way he liked it. Just about the only one who didn't do gear, but never seemed bothered what anyone

Jesus though. A man like that. Didn't look ill the last time Danny had seen him. But the others must have seen him after that, must have noticed something was wrong. Had to find them and ask them, had to make sense of all

Weren't like Robert didn't have people looking out for him. He did, he had all of us. Not like some of these other cunts, these ones who've got no one and are always looking over their shoulders. Like the old man in the wheelchair, getting taxed near enough every time he comes out the post office. Like that one that turned up at the soup run a couple of times, no one knew his name and he never spoke to no one and word was he was sleeping out in the woods. Wouldn't catch Danny going out in the woods in the daytime let alone at night. Never know what's going off in the woods, it's all shadows and hiding places and furry fucking creatures running around after dark. Anything can happen. But some cunts have got no one and they've got to find somewhere to hide. But Robert had no one to hide from, he had all us lot looking out for him. It was a what was it an understanding. Weren't it and

Laura she couldn't she said but

Had to find

Fuck

The van drives quickly now, the men in the front run dry of conversation and impatient to be done, to be home, to be off the streets on a wind-cold empty day like this, and through the darkened windows we watch the city pass us by; long dark streets splashed with light, empty parks and flooded playing fields, boarded-up shops and fenced-off factory ruins, and we see Steve, almost, dimly, we see the place where Steve's been staying, a boarded-up room above a shop with the bird-shit and feathers scraped out and a mattress from a skip hauled in and the walls whitewashed with a tin of stolen paint. A light and a television running on power cut in from downstairs. The room kept tidy, always, and no rubbish left lying around but thrown out through the window into the yard. The yard full of cans and bottles and batteries and bits of scrap he's brought back because it might be useful, because he's got a plan to do the place up and claim squatter's rights and make something of it. Car tyres and bike frames and planks of wood. Plant pots and cable and window-frames. A crowd of pigeons picking around in the corner of the yard, shifting at the sound of footsteps and flapping into the air as Danny pulls himself over the wall and falls awkwardly to the floor. He gets up again, wiping the filth from his hands and his coat, and he shouts up at the first-floor window. Steve! Steve! The pigeons swoop and circle overhead, settling on the sagging roof as Einstein barks and claws at the other side of the wall and Danny keeps shouting up. Steve it's me! It's Danny! Are you

40

there, are you fucking there? His voice cracks, and he bends forward to hack and spit on the ground, his long bony hands resting on his knees, and he stays bent over like that for a moment, a long string of bile swinging from his mouth to the floor, and he straightens up and calls Steve's name again. Steve where the

None of the others ever knew where Steve stayed, apart from Ant who stayed with him now and again. Only reason Danny knew was he'd helped Steve back there one night, dragging him along the towpath when he should have known better and left him lying in the bushes until morning. One time when Ant was in the cells. Not that he would have been any use anyway. Steve's weak leg wet with piss and drink and his arm clamped round Danny's shoulder. Only helped him out because he owed Steve from the last giro day, and when they got over the wall into the yard Steve sobered up enough to turn and hold him by the throat with his good hand and say You tell any bastard where I'm staying and I'll murder you I'll rip your bloody head right off. His voice quiet and slurred, his thumb pressing between the cords of Danny's neck like a fishmonger finding his way to the bone. Which wasn't what

He shouts again, his fists clenched by his side and his whole body straining up towards the window. Steve! Are you there are you fucking there?

He picks up a handful of stones and throws them at the window, and they go arcing through the empty window-frame before clattering into the room where Steve lies, laid out neatly on his bed, a ghost of a smile twisting across his face and his eyes closed and Ant laid out against the opposite wall, the pigeons on the roof leaping up at the sound and scattering westward across the alley and the canal and the reservoir, climbing higher over the wooded hillside of the park and the dual carriageway beyond, their underbellies catching the last faint light of the day as we peer from the darkened windows of the van to watch them passing overhead, as we look down at the zippered bulk of Robert's body between us and we remember he remembers we we

The ground a long way off and the branch in your hand a useless piece of dead wood and you're falling through the

His brother still owed him from when they were kids, and he knew it. Danny had always helped him out back then, when he could, when they'd still been placed together, when it had been just the two of them against everyone else. Sitting in their room at night, whatever room they happened to be in that night because it kept changing. Talking about ways to get out and ways to find their parents and ways to go and live on their own somewhere with no care workers telling them what they could and couldn't do. And every now and then when things had been bad his brother saying What were they like can you remember can you tell me what they were like? Which he couldn't but he'd make out like he could, he'd say They were tall and Dad had red hair and sometimes a beard but then he got it shaved and Mum was a bit fat and she was always baking cakes she used to let us help and they had loud voices they both did a lot of shouting. His brother didn't know better. He'd only been a baby when they'd been removed. Might have been true he could hardly remember himself but so what. He could remember the house sometimes but so what. Thick brown curtains in the front room and he could only ever remember them being shut. But so what. Red rug on the floor where he used to play with these wooden bricks and they were the only toys he could remember being in the house. Ants on the kitchen floor. Everything quiet one day, no one around when normally there were crowds of people in and out the house stepping over and around him and shouting and laughing and saying Will you get that fucking kid to bed. Putting one brick on top of another until the whole pile falls over. Door bangs open and people everywhere. Shouting and crying and footsteps up and down the stairs and someone picking him up and she smelt different she didn't smell right. His brother didn't know about that, he'd never asked and he'd never been told. No one had ever asked. And if they had. If they'd asked him how it felt. He'd say It's like when you're climbing a tree and the branch breaks off. You're still holding on to the branch but you're falling through

Why didn't you contact the police immediately?
   Don't know, I was just, I was in a state.
   Where did you go?
   I went everywhere, I was looking for someone.
   Where did you go?
   I went to the Abbey Day Centre, and the Sally Army, but there was no one there.
   And then you went to this squat, to your friend's squat.
   Yeah but he weren't there.
   And after that you went to

Went to Heather's place, the supported-housing place, but she never answered the door. Kept buzzing her but she didn't answer. Walked round the block and came back and buzzed again and kept buzzing and shouting up at the window. All the curtains shut. Buzzed all the other flats and got no reply. They couldn't all still be in bed but cunts never answered the door. Walked round the block and came back and buzzed again and shouted up at her window and

She was older than all of them, older than Robert by a few years maybe, and this was the first time since she was a teenager she'd had a place of her own with an address of her own and a proper lock on the door. Weren't allowed visitors but she'd told them so much about it they night as well have been on a tour themselves. Coathooks by the door, a table and chairs and a bed by the window, a shower and a toilet and a sink and a cooker and a fridge. And everything so clean, everything painted white and the furniture brand new almost and all that light pouring in through the windows. Weren't allowed visitors and weren't allowed drugs and they checked up on that so she still spent most of her time at Robert's. But even so. It's somewhere to go though Danny, she told him. It's somewhere safe to keep my stuff and listen to my music and sort of look out the window and think about what I'm going to do next. Didn't like thinking about that too long so she was always back at Robert's soon enough. But she weren't there now and she weren't

Found a phonebox by the King George and tried calling his man again from there. Nearly out of shrapnel but there was no credit on his phone so it was all he could do. And still no cunt answering the phone. Just voicemail, like anyone was going to leave a message. Always hard to get them out of bed before dinner time, cunts always making the most of their own supply late into the night before, but this was something else, it was late in the day and someone would always be on it by now. Halfway out the box and he thought about phoning

45

the police again. Got as far as some woman going What service do you require before he banged the phone down, didn't make sense what did he think he was going to say

> I found this body but it aint nothing to do with
> I climbed in and out the window but I aint done
> I don't know

And still the van drives on, and the men in the front seats talk about what they'll be doing for New Year, and the policeman asks his radio for confirmation that the photographer will be in attendance, and Robert's bagged and rotten body lies between us, limp and heavy, like a roll of carpet being trundled out to the city dump. Shouldn't be like this. Should be different, should be like it would have been in the old days, like we should be carrying his body ourselves, like bearing him high on a what on a bier of broken branches, hurrying him out to the burying ground. Burning bundles of herbs and that to hide the smell, and people coming out of their houses and lowering their heads and going Sorry for your troubles la, if there's anything we can do. They should be closing the streets. There should be a piper or a fucking what a Sally Army band or something, TV cameras, helicopters. We should stop the van now we should climb out the van and fucking raise

46

him up on our shoulders with our boots clattering in slow fury along the barricaded streets the traffic-jammed junctions and all the drivers getting out their cars and a big fucking crowd behind us as we turn off the main road and cut through that new business park with all them office workers coming out in their white shirtsleeves to watch us pass and all the drinkers outside the King George pouring their beer at our feet as a like sacrifice or a what a tribute to a life fully lived and then all the women stood along Forest Road like a guard of honour in their short uniforms and polished boots stepping out into the road to stuff folded twenty notes into his burial shroud as we keep walking carrying him high carrying him past the church and right through the gates of

The van turns into Forest Road, and the men in the front seats fall silent at the sight of the women stationed at intervals along it. We see someone talking to one of them, a red-haired woman in a black leather skirt and boots, and as we pass by we see that it's Danny again, his head lowered, trying to roll a cigarette, his hands shaking and the scraps of tobacco spilling out as we

He couldn't remember her name but he knew she knew Laura. Thought she might know something. Thought she might have seen her, said You seen Laura lately and she looked back at him and said You what? with her eyes all narrowed and dark.

47

Stepping back and still looking up and down the street in case she missed something, and her mates further down the road looking over. He said You know Laura don't you, I thought I'd seen you with her, only I've been looking for her, I've been looking around and I can't find her. Something's happened, I need to find her, I need to talk to her. Most he'd said all day by a long way and he could really feel it happening now he could feel the rattle coming on and weren't nothing much he could do. She said What? What's happened? He said Her dad, something's happened to her dad, I can't really, I mean I want to talk to her first, I need to. She said Oh fuck. She said No, love, I aint seen her. She said You need some help rolling that fag you look done in. He said You got any gear you know where I can get any gear, my man's not answering. He said I'm fucking desperate and she smiled and backed away and said Aint we all. Ask him, she said. In that car. Bloke looked at him as he walked over, looked at Einstein, slid the window open a crack and nodded like he was giving him permission to speak. I'm after some gear, Danny said quietly. Ten pound dark. He was getting the note out from his sock even while the bloke was shaking his head. Sorry, mate, he said, I'm all out. Supply problems innit. Danny holding the money out in disbelief, Einstein lifting a foot to scratch at the car door, and the bloke going Is your dog stupid or what get him the fuck away from my car, you four-eyed

★   ★   ★

48

Could feel the note in his sock as he walked away, crumpled and damp with sweat and whatever else his feet were wet with. Weren't used to having cash on him for that long. Weren't normally a problem spending the stuff but more like getting hold of it in the first place. Begging off people on their way to work, selling the *Issue*, thieving razors and batteries and meat and anything else they could sell in the pub, begging again at lunchtime, keeping up with whoever was on giro day and getting something out of them. And counting the money all the time, taking care of the pennies until there was enough for a ten-pound bag to keep them going while they did it all over again. Three or four times a day, measuring out the hours, filling their pockets with shrapnel until they could change it for gear. Having a dig and a nod and then getting up and starting all over again. Full-time job just keeping the rattles off. Takes a lot of effort maintaining the thing, a lot of fucking what, resourcefulness. The girls on the road did the best, made the most money and bought the most gear, the best gear. The sight of them there and they weren't dressed for the weather. Must be good business even today. Must be good business every single day of the year. Basic law of supply and desire and there's always a desire for that. Don't need no marketing and don't never see them going short of

Wouldn't mind a bit himself sometimes. Other priorities most of the time but just now and again.

A bit of, fucking, come over here and get some, fucking, how you like that and give us your, oh, fucking

Other things to worry about now though, such as

Down by the canal and the sickness rising in him, the rattles taking hold. Cramps in his stomach, aching in his legs his back his bones. Pulling down his trousers behind a bush because he can't keep it from rushing out, black and steaming on the frozen ground and nothing to clean himself with, nothing to do but pull up his trousers and try to do something about it later. When he gets the chance, if he gets the chance, when he's scored and sorted and feeling able to face it. Sweating and cold and feeling it badly now and where's Mike when you need him. Can't get rid of the cunt most days and now he's

Shouldn't have gone to his brother's house. Should have known it wouldn't make no differ-ence it being Christmas. If he'd wanted to play families he should have stayed at Robert's with the others. Or he should have gone and seen Laura again and made up for the time before. Probably it was too late now. Was always too late was how it felt sometimes. Already felt too late the first time he met her. Which was when, hanging around outside the Catholic church waiting for the lunch project to open and she asked him for a smoke and he actually had some tobacco so that felt like the first thing that had gone right for days, the way she looked impressed, the way she smiled when he said Don't tell no one and said I won't if you won't. Like it meant something else. Like it meant anything. Cracked red sores around her mouth which opened up when she smiled. Dark sagging skin beneath her eyes. Her face pinched and pale and her hair thin and lank but it weren't hard to think she'd been fucking gorgeous one time but not for a while. Rolled a fag for her and she said Oh cheers mate you're a diamond you're a star. Bobbing up and down on her toes like she was cold but it weren't a cold day at all. Scratching her neck and scratching the back of her head and scratching her face and when she lit the fag she sucked so hard he thought she might smoke the whole lot in one go. Obvious it was more than tobacco she had a craving for. Obvious that tobacco weren't hardly making her feel better at all. Soon as she turned away Mike was there in his ear giving it all You don't wanna

Left at the boarded-up petrol station with the weeds where the pumps used to be, weaving up through the estate between the railway and the ringroad, turn left turn right, turn left turn right, past all those white walled houses with cars parked in the gardens, and the low wooden fences mostly broken, and ugly-sounding dogs jumping up behind the thin front doors. Two lads waiting by

51

a phonebox on the corner, pacing and fidgeting and looking around so he said You waiting to score? Two lads looking at each other. One of them said Yes, mate, why, you looking? If you wait up here you can buy a bag off our kid as long as you split it. Other one said You got the time, mate, and Danny took his phone out to have a look, and that was a mistake because one of them, punched him in the face and took the phone and told him to fuck off. Nothing you can do when that happens and it was his own fault. Einstein started barking and jumping up at them but he pulled her away and legged it down the road, slipping on some ice on the corner and smacking his head on the cold hard ground but clambering up and grabbing his glasses and running again in case the blokes came along for more. What else can you do you can't do nothing always some cunt after the last little bit you

Jesus believe I'd be a generous man if I'd ever had the chance
   And what's your excuse la

Or if we lived by the sea, if we were fucking Vikings or something, we'd put him in a boat and send him out on the water all ablaze and that. Whole crew of us, all his family and friends, carrying him down to the shore with all the things he'd need for his final journey, like his sword and shield, his armour, his helmet, his what his breastplate and that, plus the women carrying flowers and baskets of fruit, bread, meat, a fucking what is it a flagon of wine and put it all in the boat with him and cover it with straw and put our grievous fucking shoulders to the creaking timbers of the boat and push him out across the wet sand to the sea and throw a match in and watch him burn as he drifts further

A what is it a breastplate

If it hadn't taken him so long to get back he'd have some gear by now. He could have been there with Robert, he could have stopped whatever it was that had happened. He'd have some gear now and he wouldn't be rattling like this. And probably Laura would be there, at the flat, and he wouldn't be chasing around looking for her, looking for anyone, looking for someone to tell. She'd be sitting on the floor by Robert's chair, tying and untying her bootlaces, talking to him quietly or getting him drinks or making sure he had something to eat. Or she'd be sitting on the bed in the little front bedroom, the only bed in the flat, the bedroom which had been hers when she was a kid and which she'd moved into for a while when she first came back to live with her dad. The room where she went for a dig because he said he didn't want to watch anyone doing that least of all her. Most people used the kitchen but she always liked to go in there. Probably Heather would be in there as well, hoping to share some, helping Laura find a vein. Sometimes when he saw them sitting in that room together, if he walked past the doorway and glanced in, it looked like some mother and daughter thing they had going on. They were the right ages at least. Heather with her arm near enough round Laura's shoulders, and if they noticed him there they'd look up like they'd been telling each other secrets. Which maybe they had. They had enough secrets to tell, everyone

Like that kid Ben, the way he was always smiling to himself, always trying to wipe the smile away with his hand. Like he had some secret that was too good to share with Danny or Mike or any of them, like he was saving it for someone better. No reason to have him hanging around with them except he always seemed to have money. That was one thing. But then he kept doing things like he would go teasing Einstein with a bar of chocolate or something, all waving it over her head and making her turn circles the wrong way so she'd fall over on her bad leg. Laughing away and making out like he didn't mean no harm. And then a while back when they were waiting by the phoneboxes and he goes I tell you what though mate you should have seen Laura last night she was well out of it, she was all white as a sheet and mumbling, you'd have loved it Danny, and I'll tell you a secret right, I'd have fucking loved to have taken her round the

When did you last see him?

I've told you that already.

When did you last see him alive and well?

Aint never seen him alive and

Down an embankment and back on to the canal towpath, falling and catching his leg on a tree stump, ripping his trousers open and finding blood when he touched his hand to his leg. Einstein beside him still, and he could tell from her whimper that she was hungry again. Should have let her finish the food Maureen had put down at the day centre. Should maybe go back there anyway. Maybe the others would be there by now, maybe someone would be there who knew where they'd gone, or someone who could give him a number to score. He didn't know what to do but he got up again and he kept walking. What else could he do. The black canal water slicked with oil and no boats out on it. No one fishing. Keep walking because what else can you do and something will always come of it in the end. Cut through the bushes into the empty supermarket carpark, and it was a long way to the road with all those cameras twitching and turning to see him on his way. Phonebox on the corner by the fried-chicken place so he gave his dealer another go, no answer again and he hung up quick enough to get the shrapnel back this time, didn't even think about calling the police he had to find a had to score he

★　★　★

Fucking, every day like this, trying to keep our heads above the water. Or more like trying to keep our heads above like boiling tar or something and some cunt always trying to push us back under the

Last time he'd seen Laura had been in her room at the hostel. Tiny room with a single bed and not much else. Two of them lying there on the bed and it was warm and dry at least. First time he'd managed to score for a few days, and she'd offered to sneak him in the room in return for a share. Seemed like a good deal to him. Got in through the fire escape and she said she weren't bothered about trouble off the staff because she was leaving soon anyway. They'd cooked up as soon as they got in the room, and done each other, and there weren't many things better than when she dug it in him. She was all frantic and fidgety most of the time, like both of them were, but when she got that needle in her hands and found a vein for him she went all still and slow and tender. Looked him in the eye as it went in. Was something else. A little piece of something like he wanted. Good gear as well, better gear than they'd had for a while, they tested out a small hit first and didn't need to go back for no more. Near enough gouching and felt good like back in the days. She asked him where he'd got it from, told him to make sure he told the others how good it was. Tell them to be careful and that. Lying there smoking, and each time he rolled one for her she said Cheers mate you're a diamond you're a star. Turned out she said that to everyone not just him. So that was something else that didn't mean nothing. To go with the rest. Her keyworker had got her the room because she was going for a rehab place in the New Year, it was all lined up and her keyworker had said she should try and keep away from the usual crowd over Christmas. You've been so strong to get this far, he'd told her. That was the way they talked. You don't want people talking you out of it, he'd said. She hadn't told no one but she was telling him now, on that narrow bed. That was something. They were lying close together but it weren't like that, he'd thought it would be for a while but it weren't. None of them had the energy or the time for that, not when it took all day just getting the money together to score. Lying on the bed and she said Danny believe, I'm going through with it this time. Which he'd heard before. I've had enough, she said, I never wanted to get into it this far, I want to be clean again, you get me, I'm going to be clean. Turning to him with her hazel-green eyes too close to focus, her voice all warm and blurred and her saying Danny you do believe me don't you?' And for a minute he'd seen the two of them some-where else, somewhere clean, a brief and lonely vision of them lying clean and healthy in a big wide bed of their own, a car in the driveway, two cars in the driveway, jobs to go to, his contact lenses in a little case on the bedside table, the smell of coffee and bread drifting in from a spotless kitchen at the other end of the house and the two of them clean and naked in bed beneath soft white sheets, without fear or shame, without scars or sores or bruises or scabs, nothing to hide as they woke to the open window of a clear new day, the breeze blowing in from outside and carrying with it the smell of cut grass, the postman whistling, the warmth of spring and all that bollocks. She looked at him, her mouth scabbed and cracked, her bitten fingers pulling at her greasy hair, and she went Danny believe this time it'll be different, this time I'm going through with it all. Which made him laugh because she'd asked him to believe that before, just about everyone he knew had asked him to believe that before. Spent his life being asked to believe things that turned out to be bollocks. I'm going clean. I'll pay you back next week. This is only a temporary situation. You'll see your parents soon. If you keep your mouth shut and keep still this won't

Went to the new winter shelter like Maureen had said but weren't no one there. Sign on the door saying it was only open after seven and even then you had to be referred. Didn't seem like anyone he was after was likely to have got themselves referred. Went round the back of the old timber warehouse near the shelter, he'd slept there a few times but it kept getting burnt out and they kept

58

fencing it off. Weren't even worth the trouble of sleeping there, it got too busy and there were too many people you wouldn't want to turn your back on let alone sleep in the same place. Always fights and worse going off in there. Saw Ant there one time taking a bloke down with a half-brick in the face. Kept hold of it for about an hour afterwards and kept saying the miserable twat should be happy I couldn't find a whole one but, the kid shouldn't have opened his

About a million things in his life he regretted, but laughing at Laura like that was top of the list. If he could take it back. If he could go back and tell her. If he could say Laura, mate, of course I believe you. Things will be different this time. Which was bollocks but it wouldn't have been hard to say it instead of laughing, instead of still laughing even while she was pushing him off the bed, sitting up and throwing her fag at him, pushing him and punching him and telling him to Fuck off fuck off fuck off get the fuck out of it. They'd still be lying there now if he hadn't laughed. Would they. But what. So what. If ifs and buts were ten-pound bags he'd have gone way over by now. And he'd laugh all over again because the way she said it, the way she went This time it's going to be different with her eyes all wide and nodding like she was a little girl telling him about Father Christmas, it would still make him laugh. It was funny. It was too funny.

Five years he'd been using and just about every user he knew came out with it eventually. Fuck this Danny I've had enough I'm going to get clean I'm going

Came out on Barford Street and back to the junction where he'd seen Sammy before, where he always saw Sammy and he was still there now. Sat on his bench working his way through those cans. Sammy mate, I'm looking for Laura, I'm looking for Mike. Have you seen them? Sammy? Sammy looking up at him slower than that woman at the benefits office. His eyes all screwed up, like the failing light was giving him pain. Looked like he'd forgotten the question by the time he'd looked up so Danny asked him again. Still had to wait for the answer and it came out one word at a time.

Not   seen
no   cunt
for

Two of them laid out together on the narrow bed but it weren't never going to be like that. And where was she now. What would she say when he told her. Would she

Mike would know what to do. Danny thought. Mike would be at the Parkside squats and would know what was going on, what had happened, what to

60

do. Might even have some gear or know where to get some where to

Didn't even need to be like that anyway sometimes, with Laura. Sometimes just, it was like being mates, like they were ten or fifteen years younger and still bunking off school and having a laugh. Like that time he needed to get Einstein some decent food and they planned it all out like a bank job, left her outside Tesco's as a four-legged lookout, three-and-a-half-legged, but then once they were in there they didn't do nothing clever just grabbed an armful of tins each and ran. Got halfway up the street, laughing so much they kept dropping the tins, and realised she was still sitting all to attention outside the shop. Fucking, ears pricked up and everything. Had to sneak back and call her and it still took her a while to come, and Laura going She's not the smartest fucking dog on the block is she, she's not exactly a genius or nothing. Things like that and it kept him going but it didn't mean

Fucking Sammy. Sitting there all day like the lord of the manor, like a watchman or something, and no one ever gets a straight answer out of his mouth. Never goes in the day centres or nothing, never see him in the benefits office or none of that. Must have like a keyworker sorting it all out. Lives in one of those supported-housing places on The Green, one of the ones for the old blokes who the keyworkers call what is it entrenched and everyone else calls fucked. Old blokes who've been drinking for years and can't hardly remember why they started. They've probably got stories and that. But we aint got the time for

Rattles trying to catch up all the time, and every day gets harder to keep ahead. Like that time the police had some big day of action with all cameras and battering rams and whatever and for about two and a half days no one could score a thing. Ended up riding it out in some old caravan he'd broken into down the allotments, laid out on this mildew-rotten mattress that might as well have been a bed of fucking nails and needles and pins. Couldn't get no rest, couldn't get comfortable or keep still for the cramps and the pains shooting through him, the sickness and the diarrhoea pouring out long after it felt like there was nothing left. Scoring the new gear after that though, that was something, that was a lifesaver, like a, fucking, a parachute opening or

When it's been on you once you don't want it on you again. People talk about detox and if that's what it means they can go to fuck. Hear that rattle dragging along behind you all day when you're blagging and scoring and cooking and fixing and it's all you can do to keep it

Funny thing with Laura was she always made out like she weren't even an addict at all. That was a laugh. That was one of the first things they'd hit her with if she really did go to the rehab, before they even let her upstairs to unpack her bags and that they'd be giving it all *There's no room for denial here, Laura, the first stage is acceptance, Laura.* She always made out that she'd got in to gear by mistake and now she was only taking enough to keep her going, just like to hold her while she sorted one or two other things out. While she sorted her entire life out. *Just enough to keep me well,* she said. Talking about applying for college courses and access courses and all that, talking about getting some housing sorted out but maybe some housing in another town because maybe she needed to move away from all the influences here. *Just enough to maintain me while I sort*

But still if he hadn't laughed, she wouldn't. *Don't bother talking to me again,* she said. *Don't even come looking for me. I don't want to see your four-eyed face again. I need people around me who can support my fucking choices,* she said, and that was mostly something her keyworker had said and she was just saying it again like a parrot. So he'd called her a bitch and a slag, he'd taken his works and his gear and he'd told her to fuck herself, and he'd slammed the door so hard that more plaster came off the wall around the frame. It was automatic. It was part of the script. Never occurred to him to

★ ★ ★

Or if we lived in a hot country we would more or less just roll him in sheets of sackcloth and put him on a funeral pyre made of olive branches and packing crates and old car tyres and fold him up in the middle of it, all of us stood around saying like prayers and that while we watch the flames lick and tease around his body and the sackcloth glowing and sparking as it fell from off him, raking up the embers and stacking them over his cooking flesh to make sure he burnt completely, fucking praying and singing as his skull opened out with a soft pop and his bones cracked and splintered into ash. Instead of this. Instead of hiding him away in a van and sneaking him out through the deserted

Through the darkened windows we watch him. Danny. Desperate now in a way only we can know, his ragged trousers catching under his feet and his blankets sodden, Einstein leaping and barking as she climbs through a gap in the fence which straggles around the emptied streets and maisonettes of the old Parkside Estate, the last of the tenants cleared out two years ago now and the demolition still hardly begun. Unless you count what the kids have done already, the windows all smashed, the doors torn from their hinges and sent sprawling across the streets and yards. Bathtubs and wash-basins thrown from fourth-floor landings and sinking into shrubberies grown wild on human manure. Black scorch-marks like smudged mascara around the gaping windows of burnt-out flats. And a great red X painted on the front of every flat to tell the contractors that the services have been safely cut off, and to tell the squatters and junkies and dealers that they can settle in for a while without fear of being disturbed. The van moves off along the road again, down into the underpass beneath the railway sidings, and we lose sight of Danny as he steps into a dark abandoned stairwell with Einstein still chasing at his

Mike weren't even there though. Got up to the flat where the two of them had been staying for near enough a month but he weren't there. Would have been crashed out on a pile of blankets or standing at the window or even cooking up but he weren't there. Weren't no one there. Weren't nowhere else Mike could be he should have been there if he weren't at Robert's, if he weren't at the centre, but he'd gone off somewhere it looked like so that's one more cunt letting him

Stairs all slipping with ice and piss and the handrails ripped out from the walls and the sickness coming on bad. Voices coming out of darkened doorways, mutters and murmurs and moans. Shouts from another block across the courtyard, splintering wood and a silenced scream. Dogs barking and being told to stop and barking some more and the flickering orange light of flames against the

dark evening sky and the sparks flying upwards
into the clouds

Thought Mike had maybe gone in a different flat
for some reason but he tried a few and he weren't
in there and the cramping and the aching and the
rattling was so bad that he couldn't hardly stand
up straight couldn't hardly walk and nothing now
he needed he

Mike had never ripped him off on a deal except
one time or two times and that was different that
didn't

Kids coming up the stairwell shouting and
breaking bottles so he went back the other

He'd had a reason those times, Mike had, he'd
told him, his voice low and fierce in his ear going
I'm sorry and that la but I thought you weren't
coming back. The kid Benny boy said you'd gone
off with Laura an that so I thought you were
sorted, an I heard these blokes you know those
blokes I told you about what I saw down the centre
them ones what have been after me since that kid
told them I grassed them up, I heard they was on
their way round to tax us so I thought safest bet
was to use all the gear so they couldn't take it off
us, plus that way if I did get a kicking it wouldn't
hardly hurt anyhow you know what I mean la. So
that's all it was I wasn't trying to shaft you, you

know that la, you know I wouldn't do that, it was just a pure out-of-necessity thing you know what I'm saying it was just, only it turned out Benny boy was wrong and them blokes didn't turn up neither, but still like it was I had the best of intentions it was out of necessity it was the mother of what is it like you know what I'm saying la

Been sleeping in any old place before they found the Parkside flats. Doorways and alleyways. A tunnel down by the incinerator where these huge heating pipes go under the shopping centre, it was warm enough in there but there were too many rats, big fierce cunts that even Einstein was smart enough to leave alone, so they gave up staying in there. Tried sleeping in the toilets sometimes but they mostly got kicked out. Sleep weren't even the right word for it. One last fix to get their heads down and then it was like no more than a blink before they were awake again and cold and sick and crawling around looking for the next score. Might have been a few hours but it never felt more than a minute. Woke in some yard one morning and found a whole bunch of dead mice about the place, frozen solid. Lucky they woke up at all that time. Some cunts don't. Easy to get too cold and not wake up, easy to get damp and stay damp and not do any fucking thing about it, numbed out by the gear and it don't feel no different anyway. End up frozen solid like them mice. Take a last dig and curl up and go to sleep and never fucking wake up.

Some bloke looks like he's still snoozing in the morning only he's gone milky-blue and he's stone cold to the touch. It happens. There's worse ways to go. But the Parkside flats was better than that. Four walls and a roof and no one to bother them. They could even leave it and come back, there were plenty to go round and they didn't have nothing to nick. Made a change. Made the days easier when they knew where they were going to sleep. Sometimes seemed like he'd spent half his life looking for a bed. All the running and breaking and shouting and arguing and stealing and it was all about getting somewhere warm and dry to cook up and get some rest. Somewhere safe and quiet and it weren't never easy to find. Don't matter how many blankets there are if it's in the wrong place. Don't matter if it's cotton sheets and feather duvets when there's no lock on the door and a mean bastard in the house. Don't matter if there's a lock when someone

Jesus but it aint much to ask

Went down the other stairwell and found a kid standing there like he was waiting for someone, like he was waiting to do business. Cap on and hood up and one trouser-leg rolled, bike leaning up against the wall. Seen him around a few times and bought off him once or twice so asked if he was selling, if he knew anyone who was selling. Kid didn't say nothing for a minute, just looked

68

at him. Asked him if he was a mate of Ben's, and when Danny said yes he gave him a number to call. Said to call it from the phonebox by the Miller's Arms and ask for Michelle. Said it was difficult at the moment, said he'd heard there'd been a few accidents and it was all a bit on top. Danny was off across the courtyard, past all the doorways marked with a red painted X, back to the gap in the fence and off up the main road towards the roundabout and the Miller's Arms and the phonebox

Weren't always easy to know what Mike was talking about and half the time it didn't seem worth making the effort to ask. Weren't always that easy to know who he was talking to anyway. Look round half the time and he's on the phone. Ask him to speak up and he goes What's that pal eh sorry I wasn't talking to you. And when he was it didn't always make sense and it was best to just go Yes Mike I know what you're saying. All this stuff about the police, the government, surveillance agencies and that. All this stuff about watching your back and looking out for who might be listening. Harmless stuff most of it but it made him pretty uptight to be around. Like when he talked about those blokes being after him, the ones he said they'd seen down the centre. They hadn't seen no blokes down the centre, not that Danny knew about. Always talking about someone being after giving him a beating but from what Danny knew they never had. Danny had taken a few since he'd moved up here, and plenty before that where he'd been staying before and then of course when he was a

Mike always going on about it but it never seemed to happen to him. Always saying something like Danny you know what'll happen if they try it la, you know what they'll get for their troubles it don't matter how many there are they'll get their just rewards maybe not right then but later I will make sure of it I will track them down and find them one at a time and they won't be so brave then you know what I'm saying not with an iron bar across their kneecaps an that not with a slab of paving stone dropped on their heads they won't be laughing an that then you know what I'm

Why did it take you so long to contact the police?
  I was worried I might look dodgy or something.
  Why would you think that?
  Just, because I was the last one there. And my record.
  Do you want to tell us about your record?
  You've got it, you can look it up for yourself.
  What do you think happened to Robert?
  Fuck should I know, I weren't there.
  And what do you think has happened to your friends?
  I don't fucking know.
  Where do you think they've

★　★　★

70

Waste of time thinking about all these questions anyway, waste of time worrying whether the police were going to suspect him of anything. Like they were going to give a shit either way. Like Robert was even going to get in the papers for

Got up by the roundabout and phoned the number and it weren't a voice he recognised, mostly they were faces you'd seen about or people you'd been introduced to but not this one. Girl who answered wanted to know where he'd got the number before anything else, so he told her about the kid and where he'd seen the kid and that he knew Ben from

Lights on in the pub but hardly no one there. Bloke in a rugby shirt behind the bar rubbing his face and looking up at the ceiling. TV on in the corner and Christmas decorations still dangling off the walls. Door swung open a minute but someone must have changed their mind because no one came out. Intercity train rattling along by the sidings, the empty carriages lit up like shop windows, the squares of light skimming over the rubbish and weeds and treestumps at the side of the tracks. The old man in the wheelchair pushing himself up the hill, the stuffing spilling out of his coat and his feet dragging along the ground as he inched his way forward one grunt at a time, each small turn of the wheel marked by a grimace across his

*   *   *

71

Huh. Hah. Huh. Keeps going but it takes him

She said All right then what you want and he said Ten dark. She said That's all? You having a laugh? He said That's all, and he heard her talking to someone else again, checking on something while the cramping in his stomach had him bent over and gasping, desperate to shit and his hands shaking and

The girl said It's difficult right now see

Einstein running circles outside and scratching at the glass

And she said Right well wait there we'll see what we can do it'll be half an hour or something and he shoved the door open and puked into the long dead grass

And we see him there for the last time, bent double on the wasteground behind the phonebox, stumbling around in circles, desperate, waiting. We watch him through the darkened glass, getting smaller as we circle the roundabout by the Miller's Arms and turn into the grounds of the teaching hospital, slowing between the landscaped embankments and security huts, round the outskirts of the site towards the mortuary buildings. Maybe in another place or another time we would be carrying his body ourselves, there would be music and prayer, there would be crowds, and carriages, and cameras. But there's none of that now. We drive round the back of an industrial-looking building and down a long dark ramp, and some metal shutters are rattled open, and the photographer records each movement as the bagged weight of Robert's body is slid on to a large trolley with a squeaking wheel by men who had hoped not to be at work today, who would rather be at home with their families, who are even now thinking about phoning and telling their wives they'll be home soon in the hope that something will be put in the oven for their tea, and as the policeman rolls the shutters closed behind us we think of Danny out there now, still walking in circles, still waiting, his dog beside him and his bag getting heavy and the sky getting darker all the time

CHAPTER 3

They lay him away behind a shining steel door in a room as cold as stone.

We gather together in the room, sitting, standing, leaning against the wall, and we wait. For the morning. For someone to come back. For something to happen.

Waiting is one thing we're good at, as it happens.

We've had a lot of practice.

We've got the time.

We've got all the time in the world.

The room is windowless and dark, tiled from ceiling to floor, with a row of heavy steel doors at one end. Each door has three tags clipped to it, with names, dates and reference numbers. The doors feel cold and hard and smooth. Two rows of fluorescent lights hang from the high ceiling on long cables and chains. A large clock sits on the end wall. The quarry-tiled floor slopes down towards a narrow gutter, and the gutter flows into a grated drain. Everything is dark. Everything is spotlessly clean.

★　★　★

And those days he was waiting there like that. For someone to come and find him. For someone to come and help. Just lying there, looking up at the ceiling and waiting. Or was it, what, sitting in his chair. Did it not even take that long. Lying there waiting for help and then all the waiting come to an end and his tears all wiped away or something more or less like that.

Which is something else we know about. Lying on the ground and looking up and waiting for someone to come along and help. In some kind of trouble. A turned ankle or a cracked skull or a diabetic epileptic fit or just too drunk to stand up again without some kind of a helping hand.

Which is when you're most invisible of all. Get a good look at people's shoes while they're stepping around you. Like they'll leave you there for days. Like they'll leave you there as long as it takes.

And how many times had he been lying on his floor like that. Over the years. Waiting. The way he waited when Yvonne and Laura first left. Must have waited weeks and months before he really gave up. If he ever did. Waking up each morning going What was that. The sound of the softly closing door. Remembering they were gone and thinking about what he could do to make them come back.

Weren't nothing he could do to make them come back and he knew it.

He knew it but he couldn't help waiting. What else could he do.

Lying in bed in the mornings, and getting up to watch television, and sitting there waiting for his wife and daughter to come home. Even tidying the flat once or twice, throwing out all the things he'd smashed up, washing the few dishes that were left, opening the windows to clear out the smell of drink so he could sit there in a state of what, like some respectability, while he waited to welcome his wife and daughter home.

Must have known they were never coming home. But he wanted them to. Jesus. Weren't all that much to ask. He wanted the phone to ring one morning, and to pick it up and hear Yvonne asking if they could talk, if they could meet and talk and like work something out. He wanted her to pass the phone to Laura, and to hear Laura say she missed him and she wanted to come home, and to be able to say You are coming home my sweetheart, you're coming home very soon.

He told Steve that one time. Steve didn't say much. What could he.

And here we are. Sitting here waiting and all of this coming to mind.

Yvonne's tense, whispering voice on the phone.

Saying stuff like I have to put me and Laura first for a change. Saying I love you but I can't be with you no more I just can't.

And then her mother's voice on the phone,

talking briskly, telling him he couldn't speak to Yvonne and telling him not to call them any more.

The sound of the unanswered phone.

The sound of the television while he sat and watched it and waited for the phone to ring. The sound of one morning when he couldn't bear waiting any more and he threw the phone against the wall, picking it up and throwing it and picking it up and throwing it until wires and circuit boards and silenced voices spilt from its broken body and were trodden into the floor.

And tidying up those pieces as well, eventually, putting them out with the rubbish, the flat a little bit emptier than before.

He could have gone there himself though.

What was he scared of.

It was a long way but it shouldn't have been too far should it. Instead of just waiting. Waking up each morning going What was that. The sound of the softly closing door. And when there was nothing left to tidy up he started drinking before he'd even got out of bed. Because was there any point waiting.

It was the drinking that had made Yvonne leave in the first place.

That's what she said, on the phone.

And if she thought it had been bad enough that she had to get away then she should see him now. Was what he thought, then.

She should see him now.

★   ★   ★

The last things to go, as the flat kept emptying out, were the television and the washing machine. Two men from the rental shop came and collected them, and he didn't have whatever it might have taken for an argument. Strength, heart, fucking, gumption or something. There's nothing worth watching anyway, he joked, as they unplugged the television and carried it out of the flat without looking at him. Mind your backs lads, he said, as they eased the washing machine down the hallway, dripping water behind them and taking a chunk out of the doorframe on their way through. When they'd gone, after he'd kicked the kitchen cupboard doors from their hinges and emptied the drawers out on to the floor, he'd sat on the front step with a bottle of cider and started to feel better. And when he'd finished that bottle, and finished another, and was lying on his back on the hallway floor, he'd realised he wasn't waiting for them to come home any more.

Which is when Steve first showed up, come to think of it.

The way these things all come to mind. When you're sitting and waiting somewhere. In a room, like this. A waiting room like any other.

We've got all the time in the world to sit and wait now.

We watch the hands of the clock tick through the seconds and minutes and hours, and we wait. For someone to come and open one of those heavy doors and roll Robert out. Bring him out to us. Take him away.

We sit and we look at the featureless door. Like, what, keeping watch.

And those hours and days he was lying there like that, in the dark, in the light, in the dark again. No one passing him by but still. Someone could have done something, could they. When Laura got out of the taxi like that. What was she doing. Or Mike, or Ben. What happened in there.

Keeping watch for what though la.

Waiting for what and these things keep coming to mind.

Heather outside the flat again. When was this. Must have been Christmas Day was it. Before she knew anything was wrong. Sort of before any of us knew. Waiting outside with a bag full of cans and snap, waiting for someone to come to the door.

Didn't usually wait long for someone to open the door so what was going on this time. Heather thought, then. She knows now, sort of. We all sort of know now.

Banging on the door, and shouting through the letterbox, and turning round to look up and down the street. Like he might have been standing out there in the cold morning light, watching her, saying her name. As if.

Banging on the door again, and the old woman with the tiger-paw slippers shuffling out of her flat and saying Excuse me but I think you'd be as well to give it a rest. I haven't heard a thing for days. They must have gone away.

Heather ignoring her because what did she know. Robert would have said something if he was going away. He would have told her first, wouldn't he. He would. He would have told her basically if anything was wrong.

Banging on the door again and the old woman still there. Saying If you ask me I'd say something's probably happened. Saying I'm surprised it's taken so long.

Heather had only talked to this woman once before. When was it. When she came and knocked on the door herself. This was a few years back. Standing there with her arms folded when Heather opened the door, going Could you keep the noise down just this once, could you please? Basically like trembling with sort of determination, backing away even while she started talking and she was right to be scared with some of the people who were hanging around the flat at that time. No one likes being told what to do, but some of that lot sort of liked it even less than most. Heather just shut the door in her face before anyone else could get to her, and the old woman probably never realised she was being done a favour did she. And now here she was giving it all Oh something's probably happened, and hurrying back into her own flat before Heather even realised what she meant.

★ ★ ★

80

And that was basically the first thought she'd had that something might be wrong. Pressed up against the filthy glass but she couldn't see a thing. Shouted Robert's name, and called him a silly fat cunt, and banged on the door. Thought about kicking in the door or something but she didn't think she could. Thought about climbing up on the garage roof and getting in that way, like some of them did, but she knew she wouldn't make it. And anyway. She wasn't sure she wanted to. Not if she was going to find something. She thought about going and getting some help. She thought but surely, a man like that, what's going to have happened to him. Thought she might say something anyway though, when she got down the day centre, if she saw someone. But probably by then someone would have dealt with it. And it was probably nothing. Because so what if no one answered the door, he was probably just asleep or something, they were probably all sort of asleep in there. So what was the daft cow on about. Heather thought, then.

So what if no one answered the door. Weren't like it was always busy in there all the time.

So how was she to know, how was any of us to know.

Except Danny who found him but that was different.

For a long time it weren't like he would have answered the door anyway. Years back. When it was just him on his own and he weren't expecting no one. Anyone at the door would have been some kind of trouble.

But if he could have just shouted.

If Heather could have done something about it, something like, instead of just wandering down to the day centre and getting stuck in to that Christmas dinner and more or less just forgetting about it.

She remembered about it later. But she was back in her room by then and what could she do.

Mike and Ben too busy going over Jamesie to think about getting back up to the flat. And what was all that. Something about Jamesie owing Mike money, but it was Ben who went steaming in and took him out from behind. Like a what like some kind of hired hand or something. Hired fist. Steaming across the lobby in the day centre, Jamesie standing by the toilets with Maggie and Bristol John and Tommy, booted him straight in the back and then clattered him around the head on his way down. Kicking him on the floor until someone got a hold of him. Near enough laughing or something.

Don't take much to knock Jamesie out. He's usually halfway there already. But Ben made sure the job got done. Didn't he just.

Everyone waiting for Christmas dinner and they could have done without that getting in the way.

Decent Christmas dinner they do there as well. All the trimmings, and a bit of drink allowed in for a change, and the place all decorated up nice. Even

Maureen letting her hair down a bit with what must be her one drink of the year or something, a glass of dry sherry and suddenly everything's hilarious. Probably a good job she saves it for Christmas. Seems like she might have a, what you call, a propensity.

Weren't laughing about this though, fucking, Jamesie out cold and bleeding all over the floor and four or five big blokes holding Ben down.

That kid though. Ben. Fucksake. Give him a few rocks and he goes all like strength of a thousand bears and that. Does himself enough damage trying to batter his way out of trouble, running into doors and walls and taking on coppers twice his size. Makes a big impression for a small kid.

Plenty of volunteers coming in for the day, and presents for everyone, and decent food. Sausages wrapped in bacon and roast parsnips and proper horseradish sauce. Don't often get to eat proper horseradish sauce.

They had him in handcuffs by the time Heather got there. Mike long gone by then, striding off through the markets with his long coat swinging, making out like he had some phone call to attend to or something.

And what was it anyway, what had Jamesie done this time.

Something about money but it seemed like more than that.

The way Ben went at him.

★　　★　　★

And Steve weren't even there so that should have reminded Heather that something was up. With Robert. He never liked being around people much but he never liked missing out on food neither. So she should have thought, when she didn't see him there.

She remembered later but she was back in her room by then. And sort of what could she do then.

When Steve was, what. While Robert was all, lying on his back and waiting. Or was it, what, sitting in his chair.

Hadn't even known Ben that long but she knew him enough that it weren't much of a surprise. What he did to Jamesie like that. Four or five months since she'd started seeing him about the place and he'd always had some kind of trouble on him. Sort of followed him like a dog he couldn't get rid of. Like he didn't know no better, like he didn't know how to avoid it. Which he didn't did he. First time she saw him he was tapping people up outside the train station, when everyone knew that was the worst place for getting caught out in one of them clean sweeps or whatever. Didn't normally like getting involved but what was it there was just sort of something about him. Crossed the street and took him by the arm and said You're better off not doing that right there sweetheart, and there was a couple of community street wardens or whatever they called them right on top near enough and he didn't say nothing he just went off with her like meek as a lamb or something.

Wardens was for dogs, when she was a kid. Times change though don't they.

Most people would have said mind your own business, called her all names and that. But Ben just went with her. Like he'd been waiting for someone to go with. Said thanks for the help. And the next time she saw him, down one of the day centres, he said thanks again, and remembered her name. She saw him about more and more after that. She liked him, she thought he was a smart kid, even if he didn't know much. Thought he was a good-looking kid as well, except his face was busted up half the time.

And where did Mike go. Talking on his phone like that. Like he had somewhere to be. Where did he have to be. Like he had something to do.

Steve was with Ant, in the place they'd been fixing up above the burnt-out shop. This is what, like meanwhile or something is it. Or even the day before. Ant laying out his works on a square of cloth on the floor. Steve feeding H and combing through his hair for fleas, checking his ears, checking his paws. Ant not talking much, concentrating, and that suited Steve. Suited the two of them.

Plenty to think about on a day like that though. Fucking, Christmas Day. Can't help it. Don't matter where you've come from. Always things to remember on a day like that. Things to regret and that. Plenty ways of forgetting and all though but.

The works all laid out and lined up. Like a soldier laying out his kit. Everything present and correct.

So, what. Would things have been different if Steve had been over at Robert's instead. He would have been normally but he hadn't been there for a few months after that fall-out they'd had. But does that make it his fault. Robert didn't need no one looking after him. Never asked for that.

But if someone had been there. Then.

We keep sitting here waiting and these things keep coming to mind. Waiting in the dark and these things keep coming out.

Steve was the first one to start staying at Robert's place, come to think of it. This was when, years back. Bloody, years. Started drinking outside the post office one morning, waiting to pick up their giros, and after a while they took their drinks to Robert's front step and watched H running around making friends with the other dogs in the street. Just sat there talking, and a while after that Steve ended up staying over on the front-room floor. Weren't like he had anywhere else to go. Two of them sat there talking all day like it was some kind of support group, like a self-help group or something.

★   ★   ★

Like no one's here to judge or offer advice or comment. All that. We're just here to listen and share so who'd like to get us started.

Jesus but. Everyone sitting around going I can't help it I take smack because my old man used to hit me or my cousin raped me or they took all my fucking kids away. Whatever they call them. Encounter groups, therapy groups, support groups. Whatever. And no one ever says I take smack because I fucking like it and it keeps me well and it keeps me fucking quiet.

Don't criticise. Don't interrupt each other. Nothing gets repeated outside these walls.

Things you have to sit through sometimes. When you're just after a script or a sub or some signature you need for something or other.

Let's just go through this form together shall we. Let's identify your needs and your goals and when we're done I can let you have a bed for the night. Let's talk about your risk behaviours before we start thinking about treatment shall we.

Shall we indeed. Shall we bollocks like there's a choice.

Who wants to open up the discussion.

Who's got something they feel they can share.

Well, Mike, perhaps you'd like to begin, perhaps you'd like to begin by maybe thinking about when you first started having these unusual ideas. What makes you think they're unusual pal. Well, they're new to me, let's put it that way, they seem unusual to me. You want to start paying more attention pal this stuff's everywhere. Well, let's try putting it another way, let's perhaps say when did you first start having ideas that you realised other people considered unusual or difficult or strange. All this, on and on, the doctor or whoever he was talking in riddles and circles while the others all talked at once over the top of him and it was impossible to make any sense.

Waiting for the hour to pass so the joker would hand over the script.

Robert and Steve, back then. Sitting there in the smoke and the gloom of Robert's empty flat. The curtains closed and the windows jammed shut and the clearing up long forgotten. Like a two-man support group or something. This was when, years back. Robert telling Steve about his wife taking off with the kid, and Steve telling him to forget about it, something like that always happens sooner or later. They're never happy though are they mate, he said, and Robert laughed and said That's about the fucking size of it.

Robert's laugh, the last time we heard it, was like a ruined accordion, wheezing and guttural, reeking of damp and ash. Steve doesn't remember it being like that when they first met, but he can't be rightly sure. Can't be rightly sure of much, now. There are too many gaps.

★   ★   ★

And when Laura got out of that taxi and went in through the window. Two days before Christmas. The things she said. She was, what, leaving him all over again. Or it was something else, like not leaving but just. What was it.

Is there anything further you'd like to share with the group.

Didn't take Steve long to tell Robert he'd been in the army. Didn't take him long to tell anyone that, as it happens. Told Ant before they'd even had their first drink together. Served in the Falklands, he said. Slept out on Mount Tumbledown a good few nights. Woke up in the rain and looked down across the sodden moorland at the tin roofs of Port Stanley, the long narrow bay, the sheep on the hill, the fishing boats in the harbour, and wondered what the point of all that was for. It was a pissing contest, he told Robert, and Maggie won, and never mind all the boys who got left down there. Near enough crying when he told Robert this, and Robert didn't say a thing.

Ant never said much neither.

Didn't take much for Steve to start crying, once he'd had a drink. Brimful with tears that he kept fighting back, and his dark sunken eyes would catch the light and shine. My country lied to me, he would say. Clenching his fists. The first tears spilling down the webbed red lines of his face. They told me to fight for decency and rights and the rule of law and all that bollocks and it was all over nothing, it was over sheep and grass and wind, it was a pissing contest and nothing else.

Is that right mate, Robert would say, is that right is it mate.

Ant mostly gouching out so he didn't have much of a reply.

My country lied to me, Steve would repeat. Seemed like every time he had a story about the army he ended up with those words. My country lied to me. Like he expected any different.

First company Steve had kept for a while but it didn't take him long to get used to it. Never would have told anyone this but one of the things he liked about being in the army to be honest was sleeping in the barracks and the camps. The sound of other men breathing in the middle of the night. Don't mean nothing like that, just, it felt like some kind of comfort or something, in a way. Some kind of security.

First company Robert had kept for a long time as well. Since Yvonne and Laura had left.

Keep waiting to hear him breathe, now, behind that door, in the middle of the night. Used to hear him breathing all the time in the flat, his lungs creaking away under the strain. Took a lot of effort just sitting there, it sounded like. Holding up all that weight. Be a long time waiting to hear him now. We know that but we stay here anyway.

With the clock, and the sinks, and the tiles on the sloping floor. Waiting for what.

Two of them used to wake up early and get straight to looking for a drink. Some days it took longer than others. Had something left over from the night before if they were lucky. But some days they were dry, and the giro hadn't turned up, or had been spent too quick, and they owed too many people to get a quick sub anywhere. Some days it felt like they spent hours tramping around town trying to get something sorted, snapping at each other like two dogs shut up in a room. Like two men in a lifeboat or something. All that water and not a drop to drink. Jesus, the thirst, the trembling, heaving thirst. Can't argue with a thirst like that. Can't stop to think whether knocking over one of the old Irish blokes who drink behind the pavilion is all right or not. Only did it a couple of times. Robert got him talking, Steve clocked him round the side of the head, and they both grabbed the cans and ran. Which was them sorted for the day. Weren't so much running as walking quicker than they usually did. What you might call scurrying or something. Fucking, scuttling. No one coming after them anyway. What would they do. Back to the flat and the two old armchairs Steve had found in a skip and not saying anything for a while until they'd made some kind of dent in that thirst. And then more or less laughing about it. And carrying on like nothing much had happened. Drinking and talking and telling tales.

Like Steve saying I was at boarding school for ten years and it weren't no different from the army, making beds and running across fields and getting shouted at.

Like Robert saying Nine years we were married and she must have hated me for half that time and I never knew, I never fucking knew.

Like Steve talking about going to India to find his brother. Saying I've just got to get my passport sorted out first, shouldn't be too complicated. And pick up these postcards I've got from him, they're in a bag of stuff I've got in a hostel down in Cambridge. They're saving it for me, they should be. And these postcards had an address on them, I can probably look it up on the internet or something. Once I've got my passport sorted out. There's some issues to resolve first. Steve talked about going to India almost as much as he said My country lied to me. Didn't he.

Like Robert saying You'd have thought she would have given me some fucking warning or something.

Who wants to open up the discussion.

Everyone sitting there looking at their feet or picking at their nails or stretching their arms out above their heads and leaning back to look at the ceiling. And the counsellor or whoever going You won't find the answers up there. Facilitator. Enabler, whatever. I'm just here to enable the discussion. It's up to you where we take things today. Why don't we start with you, Ben?

And where was Ben. Sitting in the custody suite, still handcuffed, waiting to be processed by a custody sergeant in no mood to rush. The cells full of hangovers and blackeyes and Ben starting to jitter already. Thinking about how long it was going to take to get out, and where he could score when he did. Wondering where Mike had got to once he'd sent him in on Jamesie like that. Wondering what sort of a team that made them after all.

And the same time or near enough there was Steve, sitting on his bed, watching Ant with the spoons and the lighter and all the rest of it. A bed, more like a mattress on the floor. But better than most of the places he'd slept in. Taking off his boots and laying out his socks to dry and massaging his feet with the rough calluses of his hands. Waiting.

We can all wait. Here in this room. Sitting and standing and leaning against the wall. In this cold dark room. And it's easier to think of him, now. His body in a bag.
  We're used to it already, what's happened to him. What's happened to us.

Get used to anything, after a while. The mind adapts, quicker than the body does. Even when the body can't.

See here, where the skin has fallen away.

See, here, where the maggots have eaten his flesh.

Get used to insects though, living like this. Flies, bedbugs, maggots, lice. All sorts.

Like when that bloke at the day centre went to see the chiropodist, and warned her that he hadn't taken his boots off for six months, and it turned out he had trench foot so bad there were things crawling around in his toes.

Jesus. Give that girl a medal.

Cut his socks off and all bits and pieces came with them, skin and rotten flesh and everything, and she never said a word.

What was his name. Didn't see him around too much after that. Maybe he ended up behind one of the doors in here. And who would know if he did.

Steve went to see the same chiropodist once, as it happens. Sat and waited and when it was his turn he took off his boots and socks and stretched out his feet for her. One thing the army taught him was how to look after his feet, and he always made sure he had a pair of dry socks to be going on with, always aired his boots at night if he could. Some things, when you've been doing them every day for years, you get stuck doing them no matter how drunk you are.

Nothing wrong with these feet, the chiropodist told him, cupping one in each hand and running her thumbs along the tendons and joints. You must be doing something right, she said, smiling.

Didn't forget that one. Things like that stick with you, even with all the gaps. Things like then she washed and dried his feet, and cut his toenails, and rubbed away the hardened lumps of skin with a pumice stone before giving him a new pair of socks and asking him to send the next one in. Most people going out of their way not to touch you all day, to not hardly brush up against you or even catch your eye or anything. And then that. Washing and drying and holding his feet, one in each hand. Things like that stick with you, on the whole. Could sit and wait all day for a thing like that.

Watching Ant stirring away at the mess in the spoon and remembering all this. Waiting.

Same with the hairdressers, when they go running their fingers through your hair. Same with the nurses, changing your dressings or taking your blood pressure or listening to the crackling in your lungs, they got to touch you with their clean soft hands and no one says nothing about it but it all helps oh Christ but it helps.

Same with having a dig. When someone else does it, and even the most cack-handed old smackhead does it slow and tender and gentle like. Like a gift. Like rubbing at your skin till the vein comes

95

up, easing the needle in, slowly pushing home the gear. Like in a war film when someone lifts a drink to the lips of a wounded and dying soldier, cradling his head in one hand and letting the cold water trickle into the desperate mouth.

Wait all day for that.

Can't wait another minute.

Like Ben in the cells that night, couldn't wait but he had to. Doing his rattle. Doing his nut in. Ringing the alarm and going Please I'm sorry can you get me a doctor, can you get me a script? I just really need something to hold me until I get out, please, sergeant?

The way he talks, when he's asking for things like that. All Excuse me, sorry, please. I'm sorry to trouble you. If I could just take a moment of your time. With this look on his face like, what, be-seeching. Fucking beseeching. Wringing his hands and all that. Like he's still a little boy, which he near enough is, which he looks like near enough. With his big brown eyes and his long eyelashes and his matted brown hair falling over his face, looking up at people and wringing his hands together like he was going for a part in a musical or something, like Pardon me sir and all that bollocks.

Usually works for him but. Looks even younger than he is and people go for that. Young enough to give him a chance, they must think. Like he can still better himself or something. Pardon me sir. If you could just.

Usually works for him but not that night. Custody sergeant weren't interested. Told him to sweat it out. Which meant he didn't know fuck all about withdrawing. Or it meant he knew exactly all about it, and he thought Ben rattling through the night like that was some kind of what some kind of joke.

Lying on his mattress in the cell. Curling up, straightening out, standing up, sitting down. Squatting right down and lying on the floor. Can't keep still when it's on you like that. Can't get comfortable. Pretty fucking hard to bear. Pretty fucking, unbearable.

And Steve lying on his mattress in that room above the burnt-out shop. Waiting for Ant to finish whatever he had to do to get the stuff ready. Still thinking about that last bust-up he'd had with Robert, and what he was going to do about it, and wondering what Robert was doing now. Remembering the first time Robert had kicked him out of the flat, after he'd crashed out in Laura's old bedroom and pissed himself in her bed. All the wrecking Robert had done in that flat but he'd kept Laura's room more or less intact and now Steve had gone and done that. What had he been thinking. Weren't nothing he could do to make up for that. Kicked him out and didn't see him again for years. What was it, years.

★   ★   ★

Nothing new about being kicked out though, as it happens. He'd been kicked out of school, and kicked out of the army, and kicked out of his parents' house when he went to live with them after his discharge. They'd put up with him for a month, put up with him lying in bed and staring out the window and blubbing when they asked him what he was going to do with himself now, only he'd taken the drinking too far a few times and broken a few things and made a bit of a mess once or twice. So they'd changed the locks, and told him to leave, to go and get himself sorted out somewhere. Said it was for his own good. So he'd stood outside and waited for them to see sense. In the picturesque Dorset rain. Waited a day and night while he heard his mother saying maybe they should give him one more chance and his father saying No that boy has got to learn. Took four coppers to arrest him, when they turned up.

Told Robert about all this when they started drinking together. Told Ant soon after they met.

Could have been stood there for months if the police hadn't turned up. Him and his father were both as stubborn as each other. About the only thing they had in common, more or less.

Told just about everyone that story, over the years. Makes out like he don't like being with people, but he's always happy to talk once he's had a drink. Like a one-man selfhelp group. The fucking, what is it, the talking cure. Don't seem to have worked as yet.

Who wants to open the discussion.
Who's got something they feel they can share.

Like Ben, in one of those groups one time, on a court order, and without even thinking he asked the facilitator if she could facilitate his arse. Already standing up because he thought that would get him thrown out. Everyone laughing. The woman smiling and going You can sit down I don't think we're finished yet. Going Are you scared of saying anything serious, Ben? It's all right to be scared if you are, but there's no need to be. This should be a safe space. Nothing gets repeated beyond these walls.

Ben sitting down and going No mate I aint scared.

The woman sitting there smiling and going That's great then, why don't you get us started today? Why don't you tell us about, I don't know, one happy memory you can remember from your childhood?

Jesus. Where do they get these people.

Ben told them about the only foster home he ever got placed in, with some woman called Sandra who lived in a big old house by the river and who used to wait for him to get back from school with a plate of biscuits and cakes she'd been baking, and orange squash, and questions about what he'd been doing all day. That was all right, he said.

And the woman said What else do you remember about, Sandra was it, about living there?

Which was her way of trying to like facilitate some disclosure or something.

So he told her that one night he'd wet the bed, and hidden the sheets in a cupboard because he'd been scared of what she might do, and when she found them she phoned up Social Services and got him taken back to the children's home again.

She liked that though, the facilitator. Giving it all Well done, Ben, thank you, I really appreciate your openness, I'm sure that wasn't easy for you.

Everyone else sat there looking at their feet or looking at the clock or still counting the tiles on the ceiling. And the joke was on her because that never happened anyway, it was some other foster-kid who hid the sheets and got removed, not Ben. He was there at least another month or something.

Decent place to be as well. He wouldn't have minded staying longer. He had a nice room in the attic, and if he stood up on a chair and looked out through the skylight he could see the river, and hear all Sandra's friends laughing at each other's stories. She let him stay up late with them sometimes, and they all talked to him like he weren't even a kid at all. She drank this well strong coffee out of espresso cups, and when she let him try some once he was almost sick, and when he had a bath she used to knock on the door and come in and wash his hair, holding a flannel over his face so the shampoo didn't go in his eyes. No one else ever done that.

Didn't tell the group all this though. Speaking up once was enough to get a tick on the court order. Sat there waiting for it to finish while the woman went on about remembering they always had choices and not getting trapped in the past. Ben remembered that he had the choice to keep his mouth shut and wait for the end of the hour or whatever. He was good at waiting.

Things you think about. All the time in the world for waiting and these things keep coming to mind.

Like all the stories you have to tell people when you're asking after something. When you're in need. In need of something just to hold you for a few hours. The stories you have to come up with.

Like Mike one time when he went to the church to tap up the priest, and the priest said Sit there, son, I'll speak to you after Mass. Leaving him sat there mumbling Hail Mary and Our Father and all that like he was a good Catholic boy fallen on hard times who only needed a quick helping hand to get himself sorted out. Priest up at the front telling two old ladies and Mike that In the same way, after supper, he took the bread and gave it to them saying take this and eat this in memory of me. Near enough looking Mike straight in the eyes when he said But we are not worthy so much as to gather up the crumbs under your table. And then afterwards when Mike was giving him the story, telling him that he had to get back to

Liverpool for a funeral, it was his da's actually and even though he hadn't seen the old man for years he still felt like he had to get back for one last goodbye like and he'd been supposed to be getting a lift but someone had let him down so he really badly needed the money for the train ticket and he was sure that once he'd explained to the family he'd be able to pay the money back and then some, the priest had interrupted him and said, like straight out without going around the houses or nothing, Do you believe in God, Michael? To which Mike had said without even pausing for breath I don't know Father, do you think He believes in you? And can you lend us some money for the train or not la?

This was before he met Danny. Before Danny showed up in town one day and had his teeth knocked out when he'd hardly had a chance to say hello. Because once he started going around with Danny they had things sorted out a bit better and he didn't have to go storytelling so much.

The number of funerals Mike's parents had had though. It was enough to make him believe in the resurrection of the flesh and all that.

Where was it. Under the flyover. Waiting for the soup van to turn up. The usual crowd, sitting and standing in the yard where there used to be cars for sale but now there was just boarded-up arches and trees coming up through the cracks in the concrete. And Danny must have stood out straight off, because he was carrying all his stuff with him, sleeping bag and blankets and binbag and everything, and also because he went straight up to Spider and Scots Malky and started talking to them and no one who knew them would have done that. Everyone moving away a bit and turning their backs while he got taxed, and he was off out the yard before the soup van had even arrived, Einstein whimpering and limping along behind him.

Mike followed him out. No reason for him to get involved was there but he did. Caught up with him at the crossroads by the derelict pub and said Eh you all right there pal you need a hand.

Weren't even a question and Danny didn't disagree. Looked at him with one hand cupped over his mouth and tried to say something, coughing and stumbling, spitting blood and bits of teeth into the gutter. Mike said Eh now you, come and sit down a minute, and when he put his arm round Danny's waist to help him to the kerb Danny pulled away and said Fuck off I aint got nothing left to nick. The words gurgling and dribbling from his bloodied mouth.

Three of them sat there a minute, the sun low through the evening and the pigeons chasing across the sky while the traffic stretched and hooted along the road overhead.

The soup van drove past, and they watched it go.

Danny wiping at his face with his hand, and Einstein licking the blood from his fingers.

You got a smoke, Danny said, and Mike rolled one up, and Danny smoked it quick enough that no one could take it off him, coughing up bloody phlegm once he'd done.

He'd left London to get away from this kind of thing, and it had followed him anyway. Weren't nowhere safe when it came down to it.

He'd walked out early in the morning, walked right up to Brent Cross and then waited all day for a lift up the Great North Road and this was as far as he'd got and he was desperate now. Desperate to get sorted.

You know where I can score? he asked, and Mike made him a deal.

Always waiting for that.

Always working and watching and chasing around for a bag of that. Jesus but. The man-hours that go into living like this. Takes some dedication, takes some fucking, what, commitment.

Getting a bag and then finding somewhere to go to cook it up in a spoon and dig it into your arm or your leg or that mighty old femoral vein down in between your thighs. The water and the brown and the citric, waiting for it all to dissolve, holding up the flame while those tiny bubbles pop and then drawing it up through the filter and the needle into the syringe. And waiting again for the gear to cool down. Sitting with someone

you've only just met, in a rib-roofed room with a
gaping hole where the window should be, the floor
littered with broken tiles and bricks, in a building
you can't remember the way out of. Tightening
off the strap and waiting for the vein to come up.
This bloke you've only just met passing you the
loaded syringe. Smacking at your mottled skin and
waiting for the vein to come up. Pinching and
pulling and poking around and waiting for the
vein to come up and then easing the needle in,
drawing back a tiny bloom of blood before gently
pushing the gear back home.

Wait all day for that.
  Do anything for that. Fucking, anything.

Steve still waiting for Ant to sort him out like that.
Don't even know what he's waiting for yet.

Sinking back on to the floor and Mike sitting there
saying You like that then pal while he cooks up
his own. That good for you, Danny boy? Saying
Just so long as you stick to the deal, because if
you don't I will switch on you like you wouldn't
believe, you remember that, I've done it before,
you know what I'm saying.
  Smiling and pulling a blanket up over Danny,
right over his head. Turning away, tugging down
his trousers and sticking himself in the fem.
Feeling better before the needle even went in.
Believe that pal, only thing he's ever found that

makes him feel better like that. Nothing else can do the job, and it took him two stays in hospital to figure that one out and that was two too many. All the lies he had to tell to get out at all, all the pills they gave him to keep him well, and none of it did no good. First thing he learnt when he got in there was they didn't want to hear about the details, they didn't want to know about all the stuff he was overhearing and all his what they called it his unusual ideas. None of that. They asked him about it but the deal was really they wanted him to just shut up about it. Everyone on the outside and the inside wanted him to just shut up about all of it. That's how come he was there in the first place, on account of not learning to shut up. One of the first things the other patients told him when he got in there was Stop making a fuss and learn the magic words: I feel much better now, thank you. Which he didn't though like, not by a long stretch of the very elastic imagination he had, but he got the hang of saying it when they asked and they let him split. Totally terrified when they let him go though. Mental. So many people talking at him he couldn't hardly hear a thing, couldn't think straight, thought he was going to walk out in front of a bus as soon as he got out the hospital gates. Thought the like the snatch squads or some-thing would come and get him within a day. But then he hooked up with some of the old crowd from before, and they'd got into the gear while he was inside and they told him it would help calm him down. Best prescription he'd ever had and he'd had a few. Was only when he felt that warm hollowing out inside him that he felt better, only when he felt the silence settling down inside his head that he could honestly say Now then pal I feel much better now, thank you. No one bothering him then. No one trying to tell him things and talking all at once.

I feel much much better now, thank you.

Do anything to hold on to that.

Do anything to get back to that. Keep getting back up to get back to that feeling well again. Feeling well, feeling sorted, feeling like all the, the worries have been taken away. The fears. All the emotions taken care of. That feeling of, what is it, just, like, absence, from the world. Like taking your own life away, just for a while. Like what the French call it la, the little death. And then getting up and doing it again, every time. We get up, and we do it all over again.

What else can we do.

And how long must we wait. How long have we waited already. For something to happen. For someone to come. For some fucking thing to change.

Like Laura's keyworker giving it all Change is something you need to do for yourself, Laura. You can't wait until someone else does it for you. All those sessions she had with him, going through assessment forms and working out goals and all that. I want to go to rehab, she said, first time she got an appointment with him, but he kept giving it all No but it's not as simple as that, Laura. It's not like you can get in a taxi to rehab and then come back in six months' time all cleaned up. Going on about how it was a process. Going We should start by looking at harm minimisation, we should talk about your immediate needs, we should think about getting you on to a script.

All that stuff on the assessment forms. On a scale of one to ten I feel one very comfortable or ten very uncomfortable with my level of drug use. On a scale of one to ten I feel one very optimistic or ten very pessimistic about my life in the future. All that. Talking about triggers and associations, talking about risk behaviours, talking about histories and plans for the future and trying to make sure she came along to the next appointment. Saying things like Laura, if I can get you to make yourself a cup of tea when you wake up in the morning then we're halfway there, if we can find some space in your head for things apart from drugs then we're making progress. Asking about what her interests had been before she'd had a habit.

Waiting for the appointments sometimes she felt like she was just one of his pet projects, like he was only pleased she was getting anywhere because then he could mark her up on his monitoring forms and make a big song and dance about her to the project funders. But sometimes it seemed like he was actually bothered and that was something new. He kept going on about how he knew where she was coming from, he'd been there himself, and if he could get clean and get out then so could she. Giving it all There's no such thing as a hopeless case now, Laura, I mean you should have seen me. Laughing but she didn't get the joke. But anyway she mostly kept going to the appointments. He'd said it would be a long wait for a place in rehab and it was something to do in the meantime.

Told Danny all this one time and here he is telling us now.

Doing our time in these waiting rooms. These rooms all the same as each other. A clock on the wall, hard metal chairs, a stack of old magazines, a box of toys in one corner. And always someone losing it and banging their fists against the toughened glass and shouting at the staff who just sit a bit further back and wait for Security.

Benefits office, housing office, doctor's surgery, probation. Sit there waiting for your number to come up, and you get used to it after a while. It's dry and it's warm and that's a start. That's something. As good a place to sit as any other and we've got the time to spare. Haven't we just. All the time in the world. Nothing much better to do. Is that right.

Those signs saying Our staff are entitled to work without fear of violence or abuse.

Those signs saying Anyone spitting at a member of staff will be prosecuted.

The clock ticking round and the hard metal chairs.

The clock ticking round and Robert cold on his steel bed behind that door.

Some baby crying again, and some girl begging it to just please be quiet.

And there's Mike and Danny in the benefits office, waiting to sort out Danny's giro so they could split it. Mike sitting there telling him all what's what. Going Them two you met yesterday, Spider and Scots Malky, you're best off steering well clear, they're both a bit mental and everyone's scared of them. Even the busies like. They're all right so long as you keep your distance although you've probably learned your lesson now anyway but all I'm saying is next time we're there or we see them you want to stand clear la, you know what I'm saying?

Saying all this with his hand over his mouth, learning over to mutter and spit in Danny's ear, his eyes scanning the room the whole time.

Because of the cameras, Danny boy. Can't be too careful la. Cameras everywhere and you never know who they're looking for. They can see what you're saying if you're not careful, that's why you're best off talking behind your hand, they've got lip-readers and special software and that, it's like all automatic and everything and they're

110

keeping a record of it all. Trust me Danny boy, I know what I'm talking about, they're keeping a record of it all. Danny nodding, and saying nothing, and wiping the spit from his ear.

There's a camera in here, even now, peering down at the sealed doors, while we sit and stand and lie on the cold stone floor and wait for the morning to come. For his comfort and security these images are being recorded.

Mike still talking and spitting into Danny's ear while they wait for the giro.

They'll be putting tags on us next la, they'll be strapping tags with listening devices on them round our ankles and then there'll be nowhere to hide, you know what I'm saying? Like them chips they put in dogs' necks, you know, like, what's her name, Einstein, she's probably got one without you even knowing, they'll be using that to track you and no doubt.

And then Danny's number being called, and Danny up at the little window and talking through the hole in the glass. Name, date of birth, national insurance number. Address, previous address, place of birth. Always the same. Don't matter who it is, the police or the doctors or the benefits, they've all got forms to fill and they all want to know the same thing. And none of them ever happy with you saying I don't know.

But what does it say on your birth certificate?

I don't know. I don't know.

Like they can't hear you and they keep going on, looking at the computer screen like the answers might just pop up at them. Asking you the same questions all over again: What does it say on your records? Where were you born? What are your parents' names?

Jesus. You'd think they'd have training about that sort of thing.

Like what the French call it la. The little death.

And then what happens is sometimes there's not even a room to wait in is there. Sometimes it's just a long corridor with a line of chairs leading all the way down it, with people in suits like swishing up and down and making out they're not looking at you or trying to guess what your business is. What your problem is.

Like at the courts. All these different courts spread through the building, and you find your way through the maze by following the trail of grey metal chairs against the walls. Another place where we know how to sit and wait. Don't we all. Been there enough.

Like Heather. This is a long time ago now. A lifetime ago.

Sitting outside the Family Court or whatever they called it then. Waiting to be called in, a bag of clothes tucked under the chair. Books. Toys. A long row of chairs and no one else waiting. Could have stood up and left and it wouldn't have made no difference. Could still be waiting there now and it would have been just the same. Sort of feels like she is still waiting there now.

The door behind her opening and closing and a clerk or someone coming out with an armful of papers and her shoes clicking away down the corridor. Ignoring Heather because who was she anyway.

Dressed as smartly as she could but she still looked out of place. She wanted to, most days, it was sort of the point, all the jewellery and the tattoos and the layers of torn-up clothes, but that day she'd known it would have helped if she'd just looked sort of normal and standard and capable. Capable being what they were talking about in there.

The doors opening and closing. The sunlight in the foyer at the end of the dark corridor. Felt like a schoolgirl outside the headteacher's office, swinging her legs. The metal chair cold against her skin. Her hair sticking to her forehead where she'd tried to wet her fringe down over the tattoo. Because she'd known that wouldn't help, the tattoo.

Her hair all hot down the back of her neck, and she lifts a handful up away from her head, hoping for a breeze to blow down the corridor and cool her skin. But there's nothing. No movement, no sound, and so she opens her hand and lets her hair fall and every time she does this again for the rest of her life she'll be back in this moment, this waiting in the long corridor for a door to open and her name to be called. She's waiting there now, her hair still falling from her hand against her hot red neck.

I can wait, she says.

Don't mind me. I've got time on my hands.

We've all got time on our hands, now.

But if he could have just shouted. If he could have got to a phone. And if Penny could have barked and howled and hurled herself against the door.

And look at him now.

All these gaps. All this waiting. All these things coming back into view.

Like Robert, all the waiting he did. Waiting for Yvonne to get in touch after all, to say Come on, Robert, it's been a while now, shall we have another go.

Must have known she never would.

But if she found him in that state. If anyone found him in that state. It had been too long. He wasn't waiting any more. But how old would Laura be now, he kept thinking, then. All those years. Thirteen, fourteen, fifteen. Asking questions all over again and maybe she'd come and find him one day. But if she found him in that state.

Here's something Steve, he said one morning, the three of them barely awake. This was later, when Heather was stopping there as well. When was this. The noise of H and Penny scrambling around in the hallway. Here's something Steve, I'll tell you what. This is important.

Boxes of latex gloves on shelves along the wall.
Disposable aprons.
The tag on the door. A date, a time, a reference number. A space where his name should be.
Too many gaps.
Too many, fucking, known unknowns.
That man who went to the chiropodist with the maggots in his feet, what was his name, where did he go. Is he here now.
The man in the wheelchair who can hardly move it but won't let no one push, crying out with each turn of the wheels. What's his name.
Yvonne. Where is she, even now.
Laura.

That man in the wheelchair, we know him but we don't even know his name. Plenty of stories about him though. Like he's rich as fuck, for one. Got a big house out on the tops that he inherited years back but he couldn't never bear to live there. Like he's going to leave it to some animal charity when he kicks it, some dogs' home or something. Like he reckons they deserve it the most. Like it's arthritis that's crippling him and they could do plenty about it but he won't let them get him in the hospital. All stories but so who knows what's really true and he keeps dragging himself all over town.

★   ★   ★

We sit and we stand and we lean against the wall. We lie on the cold stone floor and we wait for the morning. The clock ticking round towards the windowless dawn.

Spent a lot of time on the cold stone floor of the underpass, waiting. Danny did. Before they bricked up the underpasses and filled them in. Sat on a blanket with another one round his shoulders. Before they banned the charities from giving out blankets, before some council leader started going on about cleaning up the streets and calling it respect, some cunt watching too many films and giving it all like Some kind of rain's going to come and wash all the crap off the streets but in the meantime a blanket ban and some asbos will have to do. Sat there with Einstein curled up in his lap. Eyes down and cup held out. Very humble, very fucking what is it, penitent. Mike keeping watch at one end of the underpass. Counting and recounting the money, how much they had now and how much more they needed before they could pick up their blankets and hurry on over to the flats to score. Always starting to hurt by the time the last coin hit the cup, and as soon as it landed they were up and moving off, folding the blankets as they went, taking the steps out of the underpass two and three at a time, Mike already up ahead at the phonebox putting in their order, Danny striding past him, Einstein not needing to be told to keep up, the two of them hurrying off

116

down the street like Olympic walkers, or more like Special Olympics walkers the state of them, their loose-soled trainers flapping as they limped along the pavement and Mike explaining where the delivery would be. No point rushing because when they got there they always had to wait. But they couldn't help it. Always waiting longer than they'd been told, longer than they wanted, longer than they could bear but they had to, while Mike paced around and chatted on his phone. Watching every car that slowed down, every kid on a mountain bike, anyone who caught their eye who might be bringing what they needed. Deliver us what we need would you la. Three or four times a day, standing and waiting. Deliver us from, whatever, this fucking sickness.

Like Danny at the phonebox by the Miller's Arms where we saw him last. Waiting there still, in the dark, with the evening's trains rattling past and the door to the pub slamming open and shut somewhere behind him. Shivering and moaning and Einstein curling round and round his ankles, as if that could make him feel better, as if that could help at all, as if anything but what he was waiting for could help or can help him now.

Do you think He believes in you.
    I could just really do with something to hold me until I get out, is there anything you can do.

Pardon me for asking but if you could just, fucking.

And it was Danny doing more or less all the begging out of those two. I'm not being funny and that but I've not really got the temperament, Mike said, when they talked about it. Weren't much of a discussion. I've not got the patience la, he said. People can be funny when you're sat there like that, and I switch a bit easy, you know what I mean, I like lash out and that and it causes more trouble than it's worth. I tend to misinterpret people's faces Danny, that's my problem, that's one of my problems, I tend to see the worst in them pal and then it all kicks off. So like it's best all round if you do the sitting and I'll keep lookout and plus once we've got the cash I'll take care of the scoring is that cool with you?

Muttering all this into Danny's ear like it was a question but it weren't really a question at all. Things weren't like that. Were they. Mike was the one with the plan. That's how it was right from when they first hooked up, when Danny's first giro ran out and they had to leave the old warehouse and head out for more cash. Mike telling him the plan all the way there, stooping while they walked and spitting it into Danny's ear.

And that was when Steve started seeing them around the place. Sitting outside the wet centre waiting for it to open, reading a book or talking to the others waiting there as well, and it seemed like every other time he looked up he'd see Danny and Mike rushing past one way or the other. Mike chatting into his phone and Danny pulling that dog along behind him. Skinny buggers the both of them, needle-thin, all hands and arms and tripping over their feet, Mike always striding out with Danny tagging along behind, Danny squinting ahead of him like he was venturing into a long dark tunnel or something. Looked like people with a lot of business to attend to. Looked like they were in what you might call a high-stress occupation. Was what Steve thought, then.

There's a patch in the underpass we'll try first off, over by the bus station, big crowd from the offices coming through, should get enough for the first bag of the day. This is Mike, with his plan. Then we'll get you signed up at the *Issue*, they barred me a while back for like a misunderstanding, you know what I'm saying, but you'll be all right and they give new boys the best patches so with a bit of joy that'll be enough for bag number two. Then if you're any good at lifting we'll go through Boots and get some blades and batteries and that and sell them on at the King's Head, maybe tap up a few more people on the way back to the flats and we'll have enough for a third bag which'll hold us through until it's time for the coming-out-of-work crowd so we'll get back down the underpass and we'll be sorted in no time la. Then we'll think about finding somewhere to sleep. Full-time job living like this and then some. Takes a lot of dedication. Takes a lot of planning. Got to have a plan Danny boy, got to have a plan. Stick with me and you'll be all right. I've got the plans. Got them all up here.

Tapping at his head and tugging Danny's sleeve to guide him through the crowds by the bus station, the two of them clearing a path, Mike with his long black coat swinging around his knees, Danny with his mouth still swollen and red from the lamping he'd taken the week before.

Two of them made a pair sometimes, striding through the streets with Danny hauling a load of blankets and dragging his dog along, and Mike chatting away on his phone, giving it all No you listen to me pal youse all listen to me. Like he was talking to his agent or his stockbroker or something.

Takes a lot of fucking, what, commitment and that.

Steve spent a lot of time at the wet centre when he started drinking again. Waiting. Easy place to be when he needed to get out of the rain, and no one bothered him. Didn't have to talk to anyone unless he wanted to. And he didn't want to after the year he'd had. This was when, long time ago now. Ten years or something. Who knows. After he'd gone dry for a time, a big mistake he was more than making up for now. Which put him in good company but he didn't go there for the company did he. Went there for the food, the dry clothes, the chance to get out of the weather. He was what you might call between residences, meaning he had no bastard place to stay, but he'd learnt enough survival skills in the army to know that you make use of whatever resources are available to you at any given time. And the wet centre was a resource and a half and no mistake. Even if he had to wait outside half the morning for the place to open.

That dog though, what a state. Danny told him about it one time, said it was how come he'd left London in the first place. Some dealer smashed her back leg with an iron bar on account of Danny owing him money, and he thought it was best not to wait and see what might happen next. Keep trying to get to the PDSA to get it looked at, he said. But I don't want no one taking her off me. Else what would I do then.

Some people are never comfortable just sitting there like that though. When they're sat waiting for the same thing, at the doctor's or the housing or wherever. Think they have to break the silence. But not Steve. He could sit and wait in silence all day if he had to. Something he'd learnt on manoeuvres. Patience. Sat outside the wet centre

121

though and someone would always crack on about the weather or the police or asylum seekers and Steve would just give them a look and go back to whatever he was reading. That was enough, mostly. That and H growling at them. Weren't even a growl hardly, just this noise in the back of his throat that you knew would get much worse than a growl if you didn't stop whatever it was you were doing. He was good for things like that. Mean-looking stump of a dog, white-faced and black-eyed with a flattened nose, not exactly what you'd call playful or affectionate even with Steve but at least he kept people out of the way. Which was what Steve wanted, mostly.

But one time Heather turned up, and crouched in front of H and scratched his chin and he didn't make a sound. And Steve looked up, and Heather said You look like you could do with a drink. Made him laugh. Felt like he hadn't laughed in a long while. Felt like a start.

Knew Heather from around but hadn't spoken to her before. Hard to miss though. Big woman, with layers and layers of clothes and long knotted hair that she kept changing the colour of, and a whole bunch of tattoos including a tattoo of an eye in the middle of her forehead. Which was what people mostly noticed first. Was hard to miss.

So I can keep an extra eye out for trouble, she said, when people asked her why she'd had it done. There's sort of always trouble to look out for.

They started drinking together, Steve and Heather, and they got talking, and she asked him about H. He said he'd had him about twelve or thirteen years, since he was a puppy, and that was more or less how long he'd been out on the streets. Been through a lot together, he said, and Heather finished a can and said Haven't we all sweetheart.

She said it sounded like they'd been on the scene for about the same time. Said she'd been in a band before that, they'd done a lot of touring and it had been going well but things hadn't worked out. Musical differences, she said, rolling up her sleeve and showing him the state of her arm. All the marks from what the needles had done. Plus this other stuff, these rows of raised pink scars all up and down her arm. Helps to distract you sometimes, sort of keeps you from doing other things or thinking about other things.

She asked him where he was stopping and he said Nowhere much, and a while later, when they were leaving the wet centre, leaning out into the night like they were walking into a storm, holding each other up and slipping on the dry ground, she said I'm stopping with this bloke up the way, he don't like going out but he's a decent bloke so he won't mind if you stop there for a bit as well. And when he got there he was too drunk to be surprised that it was Robert's flat they were falling into.

It all comes round again, in the end.

Robert didn't look surprised to see him. It had been years though hadn't it. Maybe it took them a moment to recognise each other. If they even did. How long had it been. It had been years. It was hard to remember. There were too many. Could have been seven or eight or nine years, could have been two or three. Too many, gaps.

Didn't say much when Steve said hello. He'd got himself a dog as well by then, Penny, and all three of them watched Penny and H sniffing around each other for a minute, like Little and Large, growling and snapping and then calming down. H sniffing around for crumbs on the floor. Steve sat on the floor because there was only the one chair by then. Heather fell over in the corner and closed her eyes, and just before she fell asleep she said Eh now you two I'm still watching you two now. Meaning with her third eye, with that faded blue and green tattoo.

Told the same joke most nights from what Steve could tell. Weren't even that funny. Gave him the creeps.

Weren't quite true when Heather said she'd been in a band. Was more like she'd been with a band. Or like they'd been with her.

When they woke up in the morning, the three of them, with H and Penny barking in the hallway and banging against the door to be let out, Robert looked over at Steve and pushed his hat up out

124

of his eyes and said What was your name again mate? Don't I know you from somewhere?

These, gaps.

Here's something, he said. I'll tell you what. This is important.

Steve waited all day for Robert to remember who he was, and then he forgot about it. It had been a long time ago. They'd both, what was it, they'd both moved on since then. Although Robert hadn't moved far, about two or three feet by the look of it, and Steve was still drinking, was drinking again, and still going around the same places. But still, things had happened in the mean-time. Steve had been away, for one. He'd been dry, and he'd been away, and he'd come back and he wasn't dry any more. Robert had put on weight, had more or less doubled in size it looked like, like he must have stayed put in that chair the whole time since Steve had seen him. Like he'd run out of the energy or something.

Robert had seen Laura, it turned out. That was something else. Just turned up at the door one night. With a backpack and a tie-dye headscarf and some story about hating her mum and never wanting to go home. She hates me too, she'd said, I know she does, she don't want me around no more, she can't be bothered, she's all bloody

125

wrapped up with Paul and she aint got time for me no more, she's always bloody moaning about what I do all the time, staying out late and going over my mate's and smoking and all that bollocks, she's such a bloody hypocrite I bloody well hate her.

Said all that to Heather. Standing in the darkened kitchen with her backpack at her feet, glancing through to the lounge where her dad and two other men lay slumped on the floor, and eventually she said Like are they all right or what?

Heather had been drunk when Laura had arrived. But not as drunk as the others, and not so drunk that she didn't ask who was there before she answered the door. Says she knew it was Laura as soon as she saw her. Even though she didn't look all that much like him, then. She'd done her best to look older and rougher but she hadn't done enough. She'd ripped her jeans, and scuffed her boots, and pierced her nose. But so what. Her fingernails were still clean, her hair was tied back, her skin was pink and soft and unmarked by bruises or scars or tattoos. She'd brushed her teeth that morning, and every morning and evening before that. Didn't have any missing from what Heather could see.

Reckon she thought she'd come to the wrong flat when she saw me stood there, Heather said, when she told Steve about it. State of me. Bless her though, she was all geared up for this grand reunion and her old man was crashed out cold on the floor. Must have been a bit disappointing.

Who you calling disappointing? Robert asked, and Heather looked at him, and the three of them tore into laughter.

Robert's laugh the loudest of all, the wheeze and whistle of it filling the room.

Laura in the kitchen telling Heather how much her mum hated her, the only light coming from the orange streetlamps in the carpark outside, her face shadowed and urgent and her eyes beginning to shine, and when she'd finished Heather said How old are you now love?

She put her hands in her back pockets and said I'm fifteen, have you got any fags?

Laura rolling a cigarette with Heather's tobacco, her long white fingers fumbling with the thin paper and once she'd licked it shut those same clean fingers picking the strands of tobacco from her tongue. Looking around for an ashtray. Heather pointing out all the fag-ends lying trodden into the floor, and saying I wouldn't bother sweetheart it's too late for that.

He waited years for them to come back, and when one of them did he was too drunk to see it.

Should have told her to go home right then. But she wouldn't have listened. Fifteen and on the road for the first time, she wouldn't have listened to no one.

The clock ticking round and the echo of it scraping through the floor. The light fittings cold and dark.

She woke early. The next morning this was. Laura woke early, and she waited. She'd waited long enough. She sat up in the corner of the room with her arms folded around her knees, and she looked at the old home she could barely remember. She could have changed her mind then. Could have stood and packed away her sleeping bag and walked back out the door while her dad and all those other people were sleeping. She near enough did. She should have done, should she. But she didn't want to prove her mum right. She wanted to see what would happen. She wanted some breakfast, and she'd already run out of money.

He woke up, and saw her looking at him. It was confusing. Who was it. Thought it was Yvonne for a minute, looking as young as when they'd first met, come back to set things straight. And then he realised. It gave him something like a pain in the chest, a pain which near enough swelled and sucked in air as he looked at her and realised just what he'd missed and just how much he'd failed, at this precise fucking moment, to be what she wanted him to be. He had no idea what to say. She looked at him.

He got the rest of us up and told us to leave.

That was something. Never told us to leave before so we knew something was up. All of us looking at her like, what, sullenly or something. Grumbling and muttering while we went off outside. Peered through the filthy dark glass of the front door but we couldn't see nothing or hear nothing and we had better things to get off and do. See it all clearly now.

Hello Dad, she said, finally, and it seemed like such a lame thing to say that she laughed. He didn't know what to do. He stood in the doorway to the hall. He smiled, awkwardly, and it looked like someone squinting against the early morning light.

He took his hat off and rolled it into his hands, squeezing it.

He said, Look at you.

What.

When did.

Does your mum know you're here?

She shook her head. He turned and walked into the kitchen, hesitated, came back into the lounge, walked through to what had once been the main bedroom.

Did you sleep all right? he asked, coming back into the room.

Yeah, she said. Suppose.

He kept moving from room to room, picking things up, putting them down again, like he thought he should be busy or something. Like he thought there were things he'd forgotten to do. He stood in

129

the kitchen for a long time, out of breath, his hands pressing against the sides of his head, wanting a drink but suddenly for the first time in years not wanting to want a drink. He had no idea what to do. Neither of them did.

First time in years.

She listened to him moving around in the kitchen, and thought again about just getting up and leaving. She could write. They could talk on the phone, if he could get hold of a phone. If he could have got to the phone. Perhaps it was too sudden like this. What had she been thinking.

He drifted back into the room and smiled again, and she noticed how wrecked his teeth were. Half of them were missing altogether, and the rest were cracked, chipped, ground down to stumps, stained black and brown and yellow. It made him look like some kind of street urchin or something. When he tried to smile. It made him look younger, oddly, his great round unblinking face watching her, help-lessly. She watched him back.

If I'd known you were coming I'd have tidied up a bit, he said, gesturing around the room and realising before he had a chance to laugh that it wasn't funny. He sat down again, and reached for a drink.

This is, what. When was this. Long time now.

Penny appeared, struggling out from under a pile of clothes in the corner, a scrap of patchy brown hair with torn ears and a tail the size of Robert's thumb. She moved across the room like a rabbit, hesitant, almost hopping, stopping to sniff the floor and the air and anything that got in her way. Laura picked her up, holding her in one hand and scratching the top of her head, tickling her ears. Robert watched them both. She's called Penny, he said. Laura's smile disappeared, and she put Penny down again. She wiped her hands on her jeans, and folded her arms.

So, how have you been, Dad? she said, her voice brittle with disappointment. How are things? He rested the almost empty can on the floor and looked at her, steadily. Things are going okay thank you Laura, he said. Things are going fine. How about you? How about your mum?

She was gone again by the time Heather got back that afternoon, and Robert didn't say much about what had happened or where he thought she'd gone. He didn't say much at all. Give my regards to your mother. What did you expect. If I'd known you were coming.

All the waiting come to an end and his tears all wiped away or something more or less like that.

Things we don't want to remember but we do.

Can't block none of it out no more. Not now we're here, like this.

Like what Ben did that time. When there was that bloke on the leisure-centre steps eating a bag

131

of chips, and some woman going on at him. Who was he. Could have been anyone. Don't matter now. And this woman giving it all You should have told me where you were, you should have fucking told me. Kept turning away like she'd finished and then turning back to have another go. The bloke just shaking his head and talking all quietly, like he was making an effort to be polite, making an effort to be like reconciliatory or something.

Mike and Danny and Ben all waiting for a delivery by the phoneboxes over the road. Ben going How come you don't use your mobile Mike, how come we have to get to a phonebox, and Mike looking at him going Aint got no credit pal aint never got no credit.

The woman saying her piece and stamping off down the road, and the bloke calling after her, going Fucking get back here now, the woman telling him to fuck off and the bloke jumping up from the steps, throwing down his chips and chasing her down the road and then this big flock of pigeons swooping down out of nowhere and laying in to the chips, their heads bobbing in and out of the bag and the whole gang of them squabbling over every last greasy scrap.

And then Ben. Fuck. Steaming across the road and into them and they all clapped back up into the air except one slow old bird whose head was too deep in the bag and weren't paying attention, and Ben booted it across the pavement and crack into the steps where the bloke had been sitting, grabbed it by the wings and swung it over his head and cracked it against the steps again.

Danny and Mike looking at each other. Thinking what was he on, what was this, what was going on. Ben crouching over the pigeon doing, what, something they couldn't see, something slow and deliberate and they called over to him but he ignored them. And when he stood up he had half the pigeon in each hand. He'd torn it in two and was holding the bits up like a trophy and grinning all over like it was a joke, and Einstein was barking and snapping and running up and down the road. Danny and Mike didn't say a thing, except when Ben came back over to them Danny told him to fuck off. All blood on his hands and shit. Mike still muttering about it when the kid on the bike turned up with the gear. Tell you what though pal that's not normal, there's no way that's normal.

The cold dark tiles and the deep sinks along the wall. The clock ticking round. The labels on the drawers, names and dates and times. The gloves on the shelves. Hundreds of pairs of gloves, chalk-dry and flabby in their boxes.

Jesus. The whole lot of us here in a circle around him. We need like a facilitator or something. Is there anything you'd like to share with the group. How does that make you feel. What does that make you want to do. How do you think the other people felt in that situation.

Take your time. We can wait. We've got all the time we need.

Even Steve got himself mixed up with one of those groups. This was, what, ten years back, longer than that. Don't matter now. Turned out he was taking it one day at a time before he hardly even knew what was happening. Ended up going dry for a year almost. This was a while back, now.

Didn't seem to be any harm going dry just for a day, and that woman seemed impressed. What was her name. Marianne. Michelle. Marie, Marie. Worked in the charity shop attached to the project and kept encouraging him to go back to the group. I'm really impressed, Steve. Really. I'm proud of you. All that.

Didn't seem any harm going dry for the day and sitting in that group while the rest of them shared whatever it was they wanted to share and he just sat there and kept his mouth shut.

No harm except it was a bloody nightmare, the sweats and the shakes and the screaming bloody headaches but even they dropped off after a while.

One day at a time, and to be honest it was nice when that Marie in the shop said I am impressed. And then saying Do you want to come and work in the shop sometimes, Steve, it'll give you some- thing to do. Weren't really a proper job to be fair, he didn't get paid and all he had to do was mooch around in the back room sorting donations and packing boxes and nipping out into the yard every five minutes for a smoke. Marie nipping out too when the shop was quiet. And one thing leads to another and he's telling her all about his time in the army. The Falklands, and Northern Ireland, and the so-called easy posts in Germany and Cyprus and the rest. She asked him what happened to his hand, the way it was all curled up like that, and he said Ah now Marie that would be telling.

Is there something you'd like to share with the rest of the group. Well, no there isn't as a matter of fact. If I told you half this stuff you'd have nightmares for a month, or you'd think I was lying and you'd kick me out. Was about all he ever said in that group. My country lied to me and I'd rather not go into it all. I'd rather not share all that with the group, if you don't mind, he said.

But nipping out to the yard for a smoke, and Marie sitting there on a stack of milk-crates, it seemed like it was all right to tell her. And she didn't think he was lying or at least she didn't say so. And one thing leads to another and she starts on about this charity road-trip. The shop had packed up a truck full of kids' stuff the year before and sent it off to some Romanian orphanage, and this year they were thinking of doing the same only sending it to Bosnia instead.

Bloody Bosnia.

Toys and books and clothes and medical supplies

and a whole load of other stuff all packed into the back of a truck, and all they needed now was some crazy bastard to drive it into a war-zone.

Would you happen to know of any crazy bastards? she asked him. With that way she had of looking at him. Out of the corner of her eye. With a smile hiding round the corner of her mouth.

Well as a matter of fact Marie I believe I do, he said.

Weren't exactly a war-zone anyway, where they were going. He looked into it a bit, read the news reports, studied the maps. The fighting had finished, if you could call it fighting, what had happened. That was why they were going, there was stuff the people needed there, now the fighting was finished. The kids especially. Loaded up a whole truck full of stuff and then him and some bloke called Patrick set off one morning with maps and phrase books and cigarettes and cash, and the address of a guide to contact when they got there. Couple of photographers watching them go, and Marie waving him off and going Come back safe. Long time since someone had said Come back safe. Weren't sure if they ever had. Worth it all just to hear that. Was it.

All this waiting though. Still.

Waiting outside the night shelter for them to open the doors. Hanging around for hours to make sure you get your place. Waiting at the walk-in centre to get something sorted, and getting referred on to somewhere else so you can wait a little bit more. Waiting for the chemist to open to get the daily script. Waiting to score when it seems like no cunt can get hold of it, the way it was before Christmas, all of us loading up on jellies and benzos to keep the rattles off. Too much to handle if you score on top of all that and you're not careful. But careful aint really the point.

Waiting in the corridors at the courthouse for your case to be called. Waiting in the cells. Ben waiting in the cells for three days over Christmas, rattling to fuck in that concrete cube and racing for his dig when they finally let him go.

Or like Sammy, waiting for whatever it is he's waiting for when he sits in his usual spot by the benches on the corner of Barford Street. Waiting for his beard to grow. Waiting for someone to stop and talk and pass the time of day. Sammy's been growing that beard since he came down from Glasgow, if anyone's interested, which no cunt is. Had a few how you say problems and that up there. Connected with woman troubles and money troubles and anyway aren't they always what's it the same thing just about all the same. Had to come south and change the old appearance but that's years back now. And that's a fact. And now there's this trouble with the eyes, if anyone's interested. Which no cunt is. Can't see a fucking thing and it hurts like nothing else and if you're waiting for some cunt to take an interest you'll be waiting a long time.

Waiting by the phonebox for some kid on a bike to turn up with the gear. Like Danny there by the phonebox still, the trains rattling past, counting his money and counting it again and striding round in long desperate circles through the ragged grass.

Waiting in the corridors. Like Heather did. And she told them, when they finally called her in, that they should give her a chance, that they should be the ones to wait. I'll get myself together, she said. I'll get myself together and I'll come back, I know I'm not ready now but I'll get things sorted out. You wait. And the woman said Heather, it's not a question of waiting. This is a permanent order, do you understand what that means? And Heather said No, you wait, I'll get it together. I'll get myself a solicitor. I'll get it overturned. I'll never give up hope. I'll go to the what do you call it the ombudsman.

When was this. Long time ago now. Years. Don't seem like it. Jesus it don't seem like it.

She told them to pass that on for her. That she would never give up hope and neither should they. The woman said Heather, please. It's not a question of waiting. It's not a question of hope. This is permanent and irrevocable. Do you understand

138

what that means, the woman said. Like anyone could understand that. Like anyone could sort of get their heads round that. The bloke shuffling all his papers together and going I really don't think there's anything else we can do here, I think that's us done. People slipping out of the room and not looking at her, and the woman going Heather, is there anything else we can get you.

Too right there is love, too fucking right.

Her hair falling hotly down the back of her neck, gathered in a handful held away from her head, hoping for a breeze to blow down and cool her skin. But there's nothing. No movement. No sound. Waiting in the long corridor for a door to open and her name to be called.

Waiting here now for all our names to be called.

Mike. Heather. Danny. Ben. Steve. Ant. Here we all are now.

Present and correct.

Waiting at the checkpoint for the policeman to give him back his passport. On that empty road in the Bosnian hills somewhere. If he was even a policeman. The valley falling away to one side. Gorse bushes and stunted pine trees and the smell of sunbaked rock. Patrick jigging his legs up and down and Steve telling him to calm down and shut up and calm down. The guide sitting between them silently, his eyes lowered. The two policemen talking together by the side of the road, kicking loose stones away down the hillside, flicking through the pages of his passport one more time and glancing up at him. One of them making a big show of patting his pockets before stepping over to the truck and calling up through the window. Cigarettes? My friend, cigarettes? The heat in that cab, the windows wound right down but no breeze blowing through and the sweat streaming down them all. Reaching under his seat for another packet of cigarettes and tossing them down to the policeman. If he was a policeman.

And talking to the others in the cracked gloom of Robert's flat. Listen to this though I'll tell you something. This was when. Not long ago. Years after it happened. Raising his voice against the music racket going off in the kitchen. Mike and some other kid going out into the hallway and not listening at all. Robert only half looking at him and Heather saying Go on Stevo I'm listening. Bristol John shouting on about someone nicking his lighter, going Where's me bastard lighter now then. The front door banging open and closed, open and closed. A smell like pear drops coming from the kitchen, and Ben charging in and out of the room, Bristol John saying It's all right I was fucking sitting on it weren't I, and Heather saying Go on Stevo I'm waiting, I'm listening.

So then this policeman blows a big cloud of smoke up into the air and says Where you want go? Which he knew already. He'd asked them twice, he'd seen

140

their documents and everything. It was just part of the power game. The games you play when you're holding the cards. When you're holding the guns. Just like when we were in Northern Ireland. It's all the bloody same. Patrick still jigging his leg up and down and the two of them running with sweat and the guide still not saying a thing. And the policeman says You open the truck, you show me what you have. Please, you show us now. So then all three of them climb down and open the doors of this hired white truck. On this hot afternoon in the middle of Bosnia. What were they doing in bloody Bosnia. The two policemen looking through the pallets of blankets, the cases of medical supplies, the shoeboxes donated by the shop's customers who'd filled each one with a handful of games and toys. Pencils, crayons, notebooks, tennis balls, gloves, chocolate bars, action figures, wind-up cars and finger puppets and yo-yos and balls of string. A snow-globe of Big Ben with a red London bus which vanished in a swirl of snow flakes when Steve held it up and shook it for the policeman's benefit. Like, There you go boss, are you happy now. All the work it had taken to get this lot together, to hire the truck and pay for the fuel and drive all the way over there, and now these two jokers were tearing into it all, emptying out the boxes, helping themselves to a few of the things that took their fancy, toys and crayons and balloons. For their own children it must have been, Steve thought. And then they climb out, and

141

Patrick shuts the door, and the policemen give them back their passports. And then they all just stand there. The guide isn't saying anything. He's shaking. Just, bloody, shaking. There's no other traffic on the road. It's not even a road, it's just a line of gravel and crushed rock winding up round the hill, and somewhere over the hill is this place they're trying to get to. So then the policeman says.

Heather hardly even awake and Steve still telling the story. Bristol John looking up suddenly and going What's that fucking smell. What the fuck is that fucking smell now. Standing up and patting his trousers and touching the lino and going Oh fuck it I'm wet, looking down at Heather and going Heather you stupid cow, what you done? Heather looking up at him, and looking down at herself, and people coming in from the kitchen to see what's going on. Cheering, laughing. Heather pulling herself to her feet, falling down, getting up again. Going Oh fuck now look what I've gone and done. Going I thought I already went for a piss, I thought I didn't need to go again. Looking at Steve and going My cunt lied to me. Cracking and wheezing with laughter, and going I didn't think I needed to go for a piss but my cunt lied to me. Everyone shouting with laughter.
What were they even doing in bloody Bosnia.

Is there anything else you'd like to share with the group. Take your time. We can wait. Perhaps you'd like to explore some of the emotions generated by this episode. Or perhaps you'd like to keep your mouth shut and your arms folded until the time's up and you can get your script. Keep your eyes on the clock. And the stone tiles. And the deep stainless-steel sinks.

I don't know Father, do you think He believes in you.

Mike waiting in a room with one of those therapy blokes or doctors one time. Exploring the issues and all that. Going I wouldn't mind it that much though la, that's not the problem. Straight up, I don't think I'd even have mental-health problems in the first place if the voices were just a bit nicer to me, you know what I'm saying?

Waiting for the gear to cool in the syringe, and peeling back your clothes to find the vein. Stroking the skin on your arms, running cold steady fingers down the pulsing cords of your neck. Easing your trousers down and spreading your legs to find the bruised and scabbing entry-wounds along your fem. There, or there, or there. Hushed and holding your breath.

Waiting to feel the gear hit home, those long seconds between sticking in the pin and the gear doing what it does to your body and your brain and whatever else, your, fucking, soul. Waiting for all that pain to just get taken away. Wiped away, washed away. Or waiting for the meth to seep into you and get rid of that rattling for a few hours more, get rid of all the things that come up on you with the sickness. To hold you for the few hours while you work on getting sorted again. To keep the troubles away. The fucking troubles. The things that come to mind when you'd rather they didn't come to mind, certain things. Certain things which if you're not careful they all come pouring out the same way your guts come pouring out when you get sick, when you go too long without getting sorted. Comes pouring out of you. When you'd rather it didn't. When you'd rather none of it came to mind.

Waiting outside the chemist's all them mornings, Mike and Danny and Heather and Laura and Bristol John, Stevie, Maggie, Ben, necking our little paper cups of meth, draining the thick green syrup and licking our lips and Mike going Eh now if it weren't for this stuff there'd be a what's it called, a like uprising or insurrection or something you know what I'm saying.

It's the opium of the masses is what it is pal.

Steve wasn't bothered but he waited a while before he talked to Heather again. Bang out of line what she said and there was no call for it. Waited a while before he went round there or he talked to her again. Didn't bother him. But it was one reason why he weren't there for the Christmas dinner with the others. Plus it was something else. Waiting for Ant, for what Ant was cooking up.

Sausages wrapped in bacon and roast parsnips and proper horseradish sauce. Don't sort of get to eat proper horseradish sauce that often. Steve would have loved it. So why didn't Heather notice when he wasn't there. Or did she. Always been there before.

Robert would have loved it but he'd never been there for years. Never left his flat for years had he. Too scared of something. Of what. Of having his flat repossessed while he was gone was it. Thought as long as he stayed put they couldn't do nothing. Said it was all he had left and he'd fight anyone for it.

They never even tried though did they but. Must have been getting enough housing off him or something. Or must have just forgot or lost his file down the back of the desk or something.

And all the presents they gave out at the Christmas dinner, all the decorations. All the volunteers down there and it all just makes Boxing Day even worse.

Jesus. Boxing Day. One day of the year makes you miss a family no matter what. Cold and quiet outside, everywhere closed, quiet like a fucking grave. And all the lights on in the houses. And all the houses full of people sleeping it off in armchairs with plates of leftovers spread around the room and their families close by all around them. The day centre all closed up and you realise the day before was just pretend, just another fucking pantomime.

Round about then that Steve hooked up with Ant. After that business with Heather. Found him on the wasteground behind the day centre when they were all waiting for it to open one morning, helped him out and they ended up both sorting a new place to stay.

And then Ant sorted him out in turn. When Robert was waiting for someone to come back and find him that's where he was, watching Ant cooking up something new.

That's where we all were, when it comes down to it.

Except Laura. Where was she. In the back of that taxi and going where. Going to rehab, Danny says. Out to the country.

Fucking, ombudsman.

The doctor or whoever going Mike, perhaps when you feel the need to communicate with these voices.

That poster they always have up at these therapy places, going For all its drudgery and fucking sham this is still a whatever.

This huge stretch of wasteground covered in weeds and flowers and trees and piles of rubble.

Like a bloody nature reserve or something, birds and butterflies and all that and when you're out in the middle of it you can't hardly hear the traffic. Good place to go drinking. Steve walking through there for a piss one morning and near enough fell over this lad just lying there looking up at the sky. This was Ant. Steve asked him if he was all right down there, and the lad nodded, and Steve said Right then and went off for his piss. Hadn't even finished when Ant goes Actually can you help us out though marra?

And what about the rest of us, when Robert was lying there waiting for help. Or when he, what was it. Like Ben. When he got out of the cells and he could have gone straight up there could he. But he was looking for Mike. He was looking for anyone. Looking for some way of scoring as quick as he could, fucking rattling and cramping all over, running doubled-up through the streets like he was ducking for cover. Where was Laura then, when he wanted to find her. Wanted some company. Always looking for company. But there weren't no one around, it seemed like. When he got out of the cells. This was, what, day after Boxing Day it must have been, or the day after that. No one around. Like some kind of ghost-town and that. Reminded him of something, reminded him of that time he got back from school and the people who ran the children's home had like done one and there was just these social

147

workers there going Ah, now, Benjamin, the thing is there's a small problem here. A few issues. What were they called. Bradshaw. Mark and Susie. Call me Mark. They'd taken loads of stuff out of everyone's rooms while they were at school and fucked off to Spain or Portugal or somewhere. Call me Mark, call me Susie. Fucked off because it turned out some other kids who'd been there before had been talking about what had supposedly happened to them, some kind of interfering and all that. And these social workers had taken them all off to a bunch of other children's homes, asking them all these questions, going Don't worry now if there's anything you need to talk to us about. Going Did they ever make you feel uncomfortable, Benjamin, did they ever ask you to, all that.

Got out the cells and there weren't no one around. But he found a dealer he knew, got himself a bag, got himself off down the carpark basement which was the closest place he could find to cook up and he was pretty fucking desperate by then.

And how long had Ant been lying on his back in that wasteground, waiting for someone to come by and help. All night it must have been. Spent the evening drinking with some kids he didn't know, and when he woke up they'd all gone and they'd taken his crutches with them. Couldn't get far without them. Couldn't get nowhere but. So he'd stayed where he was, and waited. He'd done it before like. What else could he do. Watched the stars going out above him, the sky going purple as the night drained away out of it, the sun breaking into the morning from somewhere in the corner of his eye. Weeds and flowers coming into focus, dew forming on petals and leaves. A spider stringing up a web between two thistle stems. Moths and bees spilling out into the day. Weren't all that bad a place to have spent the night. Bit cold though but. Bit boring after a while.

And then there was Steve, looking down at him, the glare of the sun behind his head and his knob already poking out of his trousers. Great big-bellied sod with his ruined hand hanging by his side and his eyes all screwed up with drink and confusion.

Like some kind of saviour but.

The two of them hobbling out of there, Ant's arm around Steve's shoulder and Steve's arm around Ant's waist and Ant hopping along the trodden-down path. Looking like brothers in arms or some bollocks like that. Talking all the way to the day centre. Looking like a couple of kids in a three-legged race. I did have a peg-leg but would you credit I managed to lose it, Ant said. He was on the waiting list for another one but he was going to have to go back to his home town for it and it was taking him a while to deal with a few like situations. Like someone nicking his crutches the night before, for one.

His empty trouser leg hanging and swinging like a long wet rag.

Soon found out they'd both been in the army. Ant had only done a couple of years but that was good enough for Steve. Hadn't even been out long. Went to Afghanistan, he said, Helmand. Came back without firing a shot.

The clock on the wall pointing almost to morning now and our waiting coming to an end. Robert somewhere behind those doors. Boxes of gloves on shelves along the wall. Deep stainless-steel sinks. Voices somewhere in the building, laughter, doors opening and closing. Someone saying We'll be bringing that big one through this morning. All of us here, standing or sitting or leaning against the wall, still waiting. It's something we know how to do. Something we've had the practice at. We've got the time. All the time in the world.

Steve waited a few weeks before asking Ant what had happened to his leg. Waited until they'd sorted out a new place to stay, got it cleaned up and settled in. Told him about Port Stanley again, and about going to Bosnia although he left out all the stuff about what was her name, Maria, Martina, Marie. Marie. Got to the bit where the policeman shut the doors of the truck again, and gave them back their passports, and said So, now, where you want go?

Ant cooking up a big spoonful of gear while Steve told the story, and Steve watching carefully to see what he did. The spoon, the filter, the water, the citric, the handful of wrapped needles and syringes. More complicated than I thought, he said, and Ant only nodded, concentrating.

So we told him the name of the town again, Steve said, and this policeman just shook his head. Just like that. Looked off down the valley and shook his head. And he goes, No, no. You do not go there. You can not.

Ant looked at him, holding the syringe up to the light and tapping the barrel as he eased a single drop of liquid from the needle's eye.

And then, Steve said, then this policeman goes No. You do not go. There is nothing for you there. There, even the dogs are dead. Ant shuffled across the floor, rolled up Steve's sleeve, and looped a belt around his arm. Steve watched him. Even the bloody dogs, he said, shaking his head.

Ant looked up at him, stroking the pale skin on Steve's inner elbow, and pressed the needle against the thin blue line of his vein, and just before he pushed it in Steve said, like to distract himself, What about you mate? What happened to your leg? Ant smiled, and slowly pushed the plunger down, and Steve didn't say any more.

Didn't have to wait long to find out what all the fuss was about. Like being wrapped up warmer and warmer and warmer. Like being cocooned in blankets and silk. Like more than any of these things. Like being held.

We stand, and we sit, and we lean against the wall. We wait. What else can we do. We look at the clock, and we see its hands stretch towards the morning. We hear footsteps, and the jangle of keys. The door is unlocked and opened, and the lights are turned on, and the room fills with people.

Ant knows about waiting though but. We see him now, we look and we see him now, waiting for help, bleeding into the silenced ground, lying in a field beside a road with the plants flattened beneath him as if he'd fallen from the sky. None of the pain he would have expected. Not yet. None of the screaming and panic and flailing around for something to be done. Only this whispering numbness, this stunned state in which it takes him a moment to understand where he is. To understand that some homemade bomb has thrown their Land Rover into the air, has blown another hole in the road, has probably killed one or more of his mates and done who knows what to him. Lifted him from the surface of the earth and hurled him down into this field of waist-high stalks. The flower heads looking down at him where he lies, waiting. For someone to come. For some sensation to come seeping back into his body. The tips of his fingers, the ends of his toes. The blue sky. The poppies. The nodding poppy heads. The smell of smoke, and burning, and hot, baked earth. The sounds coming back with a rush, like he was being lifted from water. Gunfire, and shouts, and heavy boot-steps across the dry soil. Faces over him, helmeted faces, and bodies dangling with equipment, and then hands upon him, searching him, cutting away his clothes, touching his face. Hands which come away from his body covered in blood. Gloved hands. Voices telling him he's going to be okay. Voices telling him they're going to get him out of there. Voices asking where the bloody helicopter is, where the hell those bastards are now. Someone saying they were giving him a shot of morphine to keep him going until the helicopter arrived. And everything then okay but. The fading away of the gunfire, and of everything else. The many hands holding him tight and holding him warm and holding him safe above the good dark earth. We see the poppy heads, nodding and bowing in the breeze. We see the farmers coming to inspect their crops, walking slowly through the planted lines, treading on fallen petals, checking the curling crowns of the ripening pods. We see the farmers returning in the mid-afternoon to score shallow wounds in each pod and let the milk-white sap seep out into the warming sun, and harden and cool until the farmers come back and scrape blis-ters of blackened gum into tin cans dangling from their necks. As he lies there watching, waiting but. We see the gum scooped out of the tin cans and wrapped in leaves and laid out to dry in the sun,

153

and pressed into dung-like lumps which are sold for good money to men who come rattling into the valley in old Russian saloons with loose floor panels which open up to swallow the merchandise and go clattering away again into the hills. The sound of the helicopters in the distance. The cars grinding over the mountain passes and turning off the road by an old hill-trail, the men slinging the black opium lumps into bags across their shoulders and walking a few miles to a pair of old iron shacks beneath an overhanging rock, where boys stripped to the waist are tending fires and oil-drums and squatting over fat sack-cloth bundles which ooze dark stains into the earth. We see the banked fires beneath the oil-drums burning all through the night, the boys stirring the mixture and scooping out twigs and soil and leaves. Other boys hoisting bags of fertiliser into the drums, stirring it up and straining the mixture through rice sacks and into vast cooking pots placed over other, smaller fires. More chemicals, more straining and pressing and stirring, as dawn lights up the horizon and an oily dark gunge is spread out to dry in the rising sun. Strange light falling through the fields. Golden light. Faces set against the sky and the sound of a helicopter somewhere and a voice saying Hang in there, pal, you'll be all right. Boys' voices chattering on in some language like Afghanistani or whatever it is, boiling up a kettle of tea and chewing on handfuls of bread, pressing the coffee-coloured powder into brick-shaped blocks the size

154

of those pocket-dictionaries the officers use when they're out in the villages winning hearts and minds. Or maybe the size of those fat satellite phones they use for calling down airstrikes but. The poppy heads swaying suddenly in a strong breeze, pressing themselves flat to the ground as if ducking for cover, and the helicopter suddenly dropping out of the sky. Like a what like a fucking like a black mother goose but. What were they even doing in bloody Helmand. And all the warm hands lifting him through the air, over the field, into the belly of the mother, and the mother lifting high over the landscape, over the fields and the mountains and the roads and trails which wind almost invisibly through the valleys and passes, over the rock-sheltered pair of shacks where the bare-chested boys are bundling up dozens of paper-bound powder bricks and loading them on to dust-coloured mules who wait patiently in the midday heat before setting off in long ambling trains through the hills. And the mules keep walking steadily for days, guided by young boys who run and scramble alongside, waving sticks and shouting highpitched commands which vanish into specks of sound no bigger than the distant birds of prey which spiral high above them, following the shape of sunlight and shadow across the valley each morning until a small group of canvas-draped shacks comes into sight around the last corner and a man ducks out through a low doorway, pulling a scarf down from his mouth and welcoming the boys, offering them tea, shaking their hands like men and already moving towards the mules to untether their loads. Behind him, inside the shacks, other men are crouched over pots and pestles and fires, pounding the pressed bricks back into dust and mixing the dust with vinegar, heating it over low fires before adding water and charcoal and washing soda, cooling and reheating and steaming the solution, passing it through filters and steambaths and pipes until finally a bright white powder begins to form in the bottom of a broad flat pan, and is carefully warmed and scraped and lifted out on to sheets of paper to dry. And by the time the powder is poured into clear plastic bags and weighed and sealed, the boys and their light-footed mules are halfway home, their pockets fat with money and their talk full of what they will do with it, the things they will buy their families and the savings they will put towards a scrap of land on which to grow poppies of their own, while somewhere overhead Ant still lies in the belly of the helicopter as it clatters over the landscape, angry and low, its shadow rising and falling as he looks up at the faces around him and feels the warm embrace of the morphine flooding through his broken body while men with headscarves and rifles and rucksacks full of heroin scramble over the hidden mountain passes which cross the border into Iran, making their way down to the roads where convoys of Toyota pickups are waiting to race across the plains towards the city, tensed for battle against the government soldiers

156

who are waiting for them, soldiers who are now checking their weapons and sipping mint tea, listening to the evening's briefing, watching the sun dip behind the mountains and wondering again why they would sacrifice their lives to interrupt this unstoppable flow of wealth passing through their land on its way to the marketplaces and backrooms of the city, to be packed and weighed and repacked and sold on to other traders, other smugglers, other men with weapons and suitcases and armoured cars who will take the cargo on through the fields and deserts towards the west, to the Turkish border and far beyond, while they stay here and watch the sun dip behind the mountains, and listen to the evening's briefing, and watch through nightvision binoculars as shimmering Toyota pickups come racing towards them from out of the moss-green fearful dark. The same darkness from which the helicopter drops down into Camp Bastion, resting lightly on the ground for a moment while the many hands carry Ant out into the warm dusty air and across the concrete, the helicopter already falling away into the sky overhead as he's taken through to a spotless operating theatre where the scrubbed-up surgeons are waiting with forceps and scissors and an electrical saw. And as they pour more drugs in through the hole in his arm, pushing him over the edge into a deep dark painless sleep, he sees, in a single whirling moment, what we all can see: this strange journey the seeping poppy gum takes across continents, from an Afghan field to an English city street, carried by mules and men and pickup trucks, through shacks and labs and mountain passes, across borders, through hotel rooms and teashops and dark-windowed cars, stuffed into bags and suitcases and petrol tanks, coffee jars, coal sacks, butcher's vans, freight containers, arseholes and vaginas and crudely stitched wounds, forced in and out of desperate bodies, glued in under wigs and false beards and fake-pregnant bellies, squeezing into Europe through the narrow gateway of Istanbul and on through the transit routes of Kosovo and Macedonia and Bosnia, bloody Bosnia, shipments bought and sold by men with dark glasses at café tables looking over the sea, suitcases of money changing hands in backrooms and bathrooms, arguments settled by fists and knives and boys with borrowed pistols buzzing past on scooters, the cargo gathering weight and value and bloody narrative as it hurtles on through Italy and Germany and Holland and Belgium and France. And as Ant rumbles his way home in the hold of a Hercules, his leg cut down to a bandaged stump, he flies over an English Channel across which the heroin shipments are pouring, in fishing boats and yachts and speeding cruisers, in light aircraft, in the distended stomachs of human mules pacing uncomfortably up and down the decks of passenger ferries, in the backs of container lorries bringing the stuff in by the tonne to be driven on to warehouses and safehouses across the country, weighed and cut and bagged again on kitchen tables and workshop benches, sold on and split and sold on again, broken down into smaller and smaller batches until a bald-headed man in a baggy tracksuit gets out of a BMW on the Milton Estate, jogs up the concrete stairs of a towerblock to the ninth floor, knocks twice on the steel door, and walks in past a young man in a baseball cap who nods and closes the door behind him. And a few minutes later a boy in a grey hooded top comes out of the same stairwell carrying a bike, and rides off down the hill towards the railway sidings, down past the police station and the hospital, over the canal and under the motorway and around the roundabout to the Miller's Arms and the phoneboxes where Danny still waits, tutting at the damp ragged note Danny hands him and circling around on his bike before flicking a bag into the long grass and pedalling away up the hill, looking once over his shoulder to see Danny scrabbling across the ground for the gear and shutting himself in the phonebox with Einstein still jumping around outside, laying out his works on the crooked metal shelf and trying to keep his sweating shaking hands even a little bit still while he cooks up a fix in a blackened spoon, too much, holding his breath as he jabs the needle into the filter and draws up the coffee-coloured juice, too much, he knows it's too much or he thinks it might be but so what he wants to make sure, so what he doesn't care, pulling down his soiled trousers without waiting for it to cool and poking a new hole through the scabbing wound over his fem pushing in deeper in and feeling for the vein feeling for the blood feeling the pain the good pain that means he'll be well soon that all shall be well and he draws back the syringe a little to see the blood from the vein to be sure he's got the right place but there's nothing there there's nothing there he moves the needle he takes it out and puts it in and takes it out and puts it in and there's nothing there so he pulls it right out and wipes it clean on his sleeve and turns to the window and uses the dark night as a mirror to focus in on his neck he clenches his jaw to make the veins stand out he chooses a vein and watches closely in the darkly lit glass and pushes the needle in to a good new vein a clean vein the blood billowing back into the syringe and he eases the plunger down down down and feels the gear charging through his body's borders around his bloodstream through his heart and his lungs and his brain and it feels good good good he feels well again he feels whole again he feels sorted at last he feels what he feels warm and clean and wrapped up in silk and tissue and cotton wool he feels the way he felt when he first began he leans his face against the cold dark glass and looks out at the city at the lights at the passing cars the passing trains the orange-bellied clouds and the black star-pierced sky a flock of pigeons silhouetted against the neon walls of the shopping centre in the valley and he drops the needle to the floor and presses his hands to the cold glass and slides to the floor and curls up on the floor all this shall pass and he waits for all this to pass.

CHAPTER 4

They cut his body open in a clean white room and take him apart piece by piece.

They come crowding into the room, and turn on the lights, and open the heavy steel door he's been lying behind. The photographer from the flat is here, and the younger policeman, and the woman who combed her fingers through Robert's hair. The older man with the thick tangle of dark hair is here, wearing a black suit, and the way he stands over Robert makes it look like he's still in charge. And we still haven't got an identity, he's saying, asking, looking at the woman from the flat and another man with a notebook already out. They shake their heads, and they say that nothing's really come up, no one's come forward, there's nothing to say this is even a case. See what you can do for us today, Frank, says the man with the notebook, and they all smile and start to laugh, and the doctor asks two younger men to take Robert through. They wheel him out to another room, and transfer him to another trolley, and wheel him into a room with sinks and counters and bright white lights and trays of sharply shining tools. We follow them, hanging back a little, wanting and not wanting to see what will happen now, and as we move into the room we hear the rest of them behind us, scrubbing their hands and arms and dressing in layers of protective clothing, the medical staff in green gowns and plastic aprons, thick gloves, rubber boots, and clear plastic visors which cover their faces, the others wearing white hooded overalls just as they did at the flat, and visors over their faces, and white rubber boots.

Fucksake. It's only Robert. What can he do to you now.

They come through and they stand around his body, still safely bagged and sealed, and they talk, telling each other what they know about the case, reading the policeman's report, studying the notes.

They shift him on to a large steel table with a sink built in to one end, and taps, and hoses, and extraction fans which begin to whistle softly as they talk.

They weigh him and measure him and take pictures of his shrouded body. They switch on the overhead lights, searchlight-bright and stark and shocking. We press close in around them. We want to see. We want to touch. The policeman checks the number on the lock, breaks it open, and stands back. The photographer leans in and takes pictures, and he keeps taking pictures while they unzip the body bag and pull it open. They unwind

163

the plastic sheet from around his body, checking it for any fallen debris, any scraps of him or his life, and they place everything they find into plastic containers with labels which note the date and time and reference number, labels which should but don't say things like: a piece of tobacco which fell from the last cigarette Robert smoked; a strand of someone else's hair, apparently a woman's, which from its position at or around Robert's arm must have been there since the source rested her head against his shoulder; the blood-darkened larvae from a bluebottle fly, hatched from an egg laid on Robert's skin, which wriggled and jiggled and tickled inside him.

They take the plastic bags from his hands and his head, and as his face rises into the light we almost expect him to take a deep gasping breath, or to blink, or to say something like What the fuck's happened this time? What the fuck have you gone and done? Which is how he always used to wake up, before. With a jolt. Like he'd heard something. Something like the closing of a door, or the ringing of a phone. His eyes snapping open and his voice going What the fuck is it now before he even quite knew he was awake. His voice thick and wet and slurred. Cranking himself up on his elbows and looking around the room to see who was there this time, waiting for someone to catch his eye and saying Will someone get me a fucking drink or what?

They take photographs. They cut slices from the ends of his cracked yellow fingernails and drop them into labelled plastic bags. They pluck hairs from the top of his head, from his eyebrows, from his nostrils, tearing them out by the root and dropping them into more labelled bags.

Should be more like this though but. We drape a freshly laundered sheet across a long wooden table and lay him out on that, dressed in his Sunday best. We put his head on a soft silk cushion. We weigh his eyelids down with pennies, and stuff his arse with cotton wool. We place flowers around him, and light candles, and put out chairs so that people can come and go all through the day and night to remember who he was and how he was and raise a drink and tell stories about his long eventful life. Like a what they call it a wake. Like saying remember this.

Remember the woman cutting hair at the day centre. Every couple of weeks she'd be there, with her combs and scissors and bottles of shampoo. Weren't bothered about keeping it short or how it looked to be honest but just, being touched. Hands running through your hair. Someone taking the time. Someone holding up a mirror and asking if that was okay. Worth waiting for. Robert never went down there, never went anywhere, borrowed Steve's clippers every few months and buzzcut it himself, made a right mess of it most times as it happens but no one ever said. Could do with someone trimming his hair nice now and not just tearing it out by the root.

And what about. All the cigarettes that have stained those fingernails. The layers of grease and dust and skin which have collected beneath them. Each moment of his life scraped up under there. The fabric of the armchair worn thin beneath his fidgeting hands. The labels of beer-bottles picked away from the cold wet glass. The way he would scratch at Yvonne's back sometimes, when they were in bed together, each sharpened caress making her arch and shriek above him, and the way afterwards she would peer over her shoulder to see the marks he'd left on her, and laugh proudly, and call him a mean bastard, smiling as she said it, and roll off the bed to look for their cigarettes. The sight of her skinny arse as she walked away from the bed like that. Fucking, what was it. The two of them smoking together then, and later, once she'd left, the two of them smoking apart, in rooms a hundred miles away, their fingers yellowing and the memory of each other flaring to life each time they lit up, no matter what they did to avoid it, the drinking and whatever else. The way memories like that end up a part of you, and then pop out again with some movement or some bang on the bone. For example what. For example the number of times, years after she left, he would take his first drag on a cigarette and then find himself holding it out in mid-air, offering it to someone who wasn't there. Who hadn't been there for years. For example the way, in those first few months together, she'd only take a few drags

166

before stubbing it out and wrestling him on to his back for another go. Fucking Yvonne. Where did she come from. Where the fuck did she go. And the blood beneath his fingernails that time, the only time. When he lashed out at her by mistake. He'd only wanted to warn her, but she'd moved at the last moment, and he'd caught her awkwardly, caught the skin just by her eye with his fingernails, felt the skin tearing he thought. And there was the blood on his nails, a tiny spot, a tiny fucking damn spot. It was only the one time, weren't it. And it had been more or less a mistake. The pain in his head. Just a slap, fucking, not even a slap. Because if she hadn't moved at the last minute. But the way she'd looked at him then, like something had closed off inside her. And her cheek, around where he'd caught her. Red. The ragged edges of the broken skin. The way she said You bastard, without smiling, without room for him to say anything back. Running the taps in the bathroom, and the smell of cigarette smoke curling out while he stood there and knocked on the door. Her muffled voice telling him he had to go and collect Laura from the school because she wasn't going in this state.

Only the one time. Weren't it.

There are things we didn't know before, and we know them now. How but. These things coming to us slowly, surely, rising to the surface like bruises and scars.

Never seen him still like this before. Have you.

Even when he was asleep he was all fidgeting and scratching and muttering on, rolling over, pulling at whatever jacket or blanket he'd hauled over himself when he crashed to the floor. And when he was awake he never sat still. Never left the flat but he couldn't stop moving. Getting a drink, rolling a fag, going over to the window, going for a piss, scratching and talking and waving his arms around to make a point. Telling someone to clear their shit up, telling someone to get him some snap. Telling a story or just sitting there shaking and trembling like there was a current running through him, waiting for a drink. So maybe this is some kind of peace, this stillness he's got himself now. Maybe you can call it that, at least.

Remember his fingernails though. Do you. Cracked, yellow, bitten-down. And now they're clipped off and dropped into clear plastic pouches. Put them under a microscope and see what stories they tell. And Laura's fingernails, that first time she came knocking on Robert's door, remember Heather couldn't stop looking at them, couldn't believe them, long and clean and curved at the ends. Polished. The fingernails of a girl with a clean bathroom where there are handcreams and nail scissors and emery boards and a neat row of clear and coloured varnishes lined up on the shelves. Sort of made Heather think of when she was younger, like much younger, when she first went out on the road with the band, when she was still looking after herself. Laura had ripped her jeans and put on these big clumpy boots but her nails still gave her away. The look on Robert's face when he woke up next morning and saw her there, and then the look on his face when she went straight off again. Sort of like he couldn't tell if he'd dreamt it or what. Those perfect fingernails, those long white fingers, clean fingers, Heather had wanted to take the girl's hand and hold it against her face. Had a feeling like that would be nice. Laura had that effect on people, then. It was unsettling. They weren't used to it. Wanted to put one of those clean white fingers in her mouth. The taste of it.

The old man, the doctor or whoever he is, speaks to a younger man who writes his words down on a whiteboard on the wall, and a woman with clipped-back hair and black-rimmed glasses starts to cut into Robert's clothes. Black fleece, the doctor says, greasy stains to cuffs and neck, cigarette burns or similar on chest area, large rip approximately, what, one hundred and seventy millimetres, running up from left waist. The photographer leans in to get pictures of all this, and someone else places a ruler next to the rip in Robert's filthy clothes.

That's all those times he fell asleep with a fag on the go, the drinks he spilt over himself. That's the fight he had with Steve a couple of months back. When he pulled away from Steve and his fleece ripped up the side where Steve was holding it. Weren't hardly a fight though, it was mostly just holding on, banging heads and swinging elbows and holding each other up. Didn't come out of much and didn't look like it was going that far until Steve took a bite on Robert's ear. Remember that. Just leant round and took a bite, and once Robert had pulled away and made sure his ear was still there he kicked right off. Didn't he. Remember. Weren't much of a fight after that. A man the size of Robert, once he puts his mind to it he's like a what is it a force to be reckoned with a force of nature. Pushing and punching Steve out through the front door and down the steps and shouting all this stuff like You fucking headcase you cunt you can fuck right off and all that. Kept putting his hand to his ear to make sure it was all there or something and spitting out blood where Steve had caught him in the mouth. Rolling up his hat and holding it against his ear. Someone found H and brought him out, and someone else got Steve's coat and threw it over him where he lay, and Robert started looking up and down the street like he'd only just realised he was outside. Was the first time he'd been outside for a while, and it was the last time until those blokes with the stretcher and the black van carried him out.

Reckon that was the last time Steve was there anyways. unless. Unless what. Some things we don't know yet. Steve and H stumbling off down the street without looking back, Steve pulling his coat on and rubbing at his knuckles where he'd caught Robert in the mouth. Robert backing away into the flat going What the fuck was all that about and looking for another drink. Pushing his hat back over his head. The two of them picking away at each other all day but it still seemed to come out of nowhere. Robert saying something about Steve never being a real soldier and Steve standing over him going Say that again, and Robert standing up and the two of them going at it. The closeness of them, in that moment, breathing into each other, the sharp smack of knuckle on bone and their faces pressing and scratching together, the smell of drink and cold sweat and the first taste of blood in the mouth, the unfocused stare in the eyes. The dense metallic ring of each punch as it fell. Steve's teeth biting on his ear, and the crunch of pain that followed. Steve saying, even while Robert was knocking him out of the door, Don't you ever say that about me again, that was nothing mate, you say that again and you see what happens, I was a soldier you bastard, I served my country you bastard. Lying curled up at the bottom of the steps going I served my country, and Ben hurling his coat down over him and laughing and telling him to shut up. Booting him one in the ribs just for fun. Robert touching his ear and turning away into the flat. Don't mean nothing now. But if he knew. If Robert knew, if he'd taken the trouble to ask, if he'd given Steve the chance to tell him all the things he'd seen and done when he was away with the army, then he wouldn't have said that, he wouldn't have dared, it wouldn't ever have occurred to him to say something like that. Steve's done his time and that's the God's honest truth. In Belfast, peering out through the letterbox windows of the Land Rover, rocks and bottles raining down, his gun heavy in his lap and the taste of bile in his mouth, ready to rattle out through those back doors and take up positions, waving shields and sticks and shouting Get back, get back, you bastards, get back. Petrol bombs splashing and flaming around their feet, stones and lumps of iron falling from the sky. Gunfire. From nowhere, from bloody everywhere, gunfire. Scanning the rooftops, the windows, the alley-entrances. More gunfire, and a man down beside him, Craigie, his leg ripped open and blood gushing out on to the road. I mean just literally gushing. The shouts of Man down, and idiot whooping in the crowd, and our guns raised in their faces Now will you bloody get back or what, bloody get back. And down in Armagh, wading across sodden meadows and scrambling through ditches, rainwater gushing into drains and culverts like the blood from Craigie's leg on that road and in the back of the Land Rover and some poor bastard had to swab that out when it was all done. Never told me I'd be doing that. My country lied to me. If Robert had known any of that, if he'd ever listened, if anyone ever listened, he wouldn't have made something of it like that, he wouldn't have said what he did. If he knew. Would he.

The woman with the black-rimmed glasses takes a large pair of blunt-nosed scissors and cuts the fleece open up the middle, turning and cutting along each sleeve and peeling the layers apart. She stands back for the photographer to get another shot, and the doctor asks the younger man at the whiteboard to make another note about staining to a long-sleeved undergarment, and again the scissors cut a line up the middle and along each sleeve, and again the layers are peeled back with a soft wet unsticking sound. They cut through a shirt, a couple of t-shirts, and a vest, and it takes us a moment to realise that the blackened surface beneath all these layers, shining wetly under the lights, is his broad and swollen chest. They cut away his trousers, and the material falls off him like sodden rags. They cut away his socks, and the soiled remains of his pants, and he lies before us, between us, naked, beaten. We move closer. We reach out our hands.

They lift him by the shoulders and slide a thick rubber block beneath his back, pushing his chest up and his head back and stretching out his arms, and the woman with the black-rimmed glasses uncoils a length of hose from one end of the table and begins to wash him down, the water streaming gently across his bloated body, down into the gullies which run along either side of the table

173

and into a sink and drain at the far end. The water runs slowly, softly. We wonder whether it's warm. She rinses him all over, using soap pads to work away the dirt and blood which remains. She begins with his fingers, wiping down to the cleft between each one and across his palms and the backs of his hands, encircling his wrist and lifting each arm as she draws the pads along his forearm and elbow and up to his shoulder. She lowers each arm gently, softly, as if being careful not to wake him. With a clean pad she burrows, delicately, into the thick matted hair of his armpits.

She cleans his chest and stomach, his hips, his thighs and shins and feet, running the pads across his body in broad sweeping gestures. She takes swabs from his mouth and nose and ears, his anus, the tip of his penis. She wipes his neck, his face, his lips, the lids of his eyes. She cleans around his groin, lifting the swollen weight of his penis and his balls while she works around each fold of skin, and then the others help to tilt him up on to his side so she can clean his back and buttocks and the underneath of his thighs.

Nearest he's come to a bath in years.

Robert and Laura in the bath together. Years ago, before anything fell apart. Laura laughing at the strange black hair sprouting all over him and daring to touch it. I've only got hair on my head, she says, looking down at herself, and you've got it all over that's funny. Her small smooth body so strange, her head brimming over with questions and talk, and after they'd gone he tried to remember when she'd stopped talking to him like that, when she'd looked away and not sat in his lap and acted as though he was someone to be afraid around. He'd done nothing to be afraid of. Had he. It was only the way Yvonne behaved, the things she told her. The sight of her shrinking away from him, the shocking way a child can do that, making herself small and out of reach and making his hands hang uselessly by his side.

And remember that second time Laura came home to her dad's. How she was shocked all over again by how much he'd changed. Remember that. Fatter, redder, more bruised and falling-down. She should see him now. She should but where is she. Would she look at him now, would she shrink away. His skin broken and rotting, his flesh a mottled mess of red and black and purple and cream. His nakedness stripped of meaning. His wounds and scars noted down by people who don't even know his name.

Feet: advanced state of decay, presumably predating death. Bruising to both shins, knees, upper thighs, hips. Faded scar on right thigh. The younger man writes all this down, and the photographer takes more pictures, and the others crowd around and look.

Blackening of skin to the back of torso, buttocks, and backs of legs, consistent with the subject having remained in a prone position, face-upwards, for a period of days following death. Bruising around ribs. Bruising to left side of face. No scratches or bruises to hands or forearms.

The crowd of them shuffling around his body, peering and pointing as they write these things down. We move closer. We want to touch, we want to touch him. Mike hangs back a little and tells us, by the way, like it don't mean nothing, that he's not sure but he maybe might have been the last one there before Robert died. Don't matter no more anyhow la but it's just worth mentioning. He tells us he didn't do nothing or nothing he was just there. He tells us he's only just thought of it like.

Robert was still in the kitchen when he left so it can't have been nothing to do with him but it don't matter no more anyhow. Mike tells us now.

The man with the notebook who looks like a policeman or a detective or something says, So what's going on with these bruises, Frank? and the doctor says I think I'll let my very capable junior here answer that. The younger man by the whiteboard looks up and says They're probably all falls and bumps, aren't they? The doctor smiles, and nods, and the detective puts his notebook away. From the pictures of the scene, we're probably going to find that he was an alcoholic, the younger man continues, and alcoholics tend to fall over a lot and bruise very easily. And there's nothing here which looks like a defensive injury.

The doctor, Frank, nods again, gesturing to the younger man and saying This is my junior in whom I am most pleased. They all laugh, and the detective leaves the room. Give me a shout if you find a bullet hole, he says, as he goes.

All of us sitting around with the candles and music and flowers and that, and when it all goes quiet someone says Eh but the undertakers have done a lovely job haven't they but? He looks smashing and that. He looks better than he has done for years, someone else says, and we laugh, and we think about more of the times we spent with him.

Think about how after the fight that time there was Steve and H stamping off down the street, going That stupid bastard who does he bloody well think he is. Went down to the corner shop by the rec and stocked up on Storm, spent the rest of the week's giro in one go and lugged it all down to the corner of Barford Street, down to Sammy's patch, sat on the benches with Sammy down there for the rest of the day. Told him what Robert had said, what had happened, about that bloody little sod Ben running out and joining in, the little sod, what does he even know about anything. Sammy weren't even listening anyway. Never does. Just sat there drinking a bottle of vodka with no label he'd got from who knows where. Some Polish bollocks, he said, or Russian or one of them. Wouldn't let Steve have none anyway. Was there most of the rest of the day and he didn't say much, just Aye pal when Steve kept talking about what Robert had said, how he wouldn't have said it if he knew where Steve had been and what he'd done, if he really knew what Steve had seen. Saying I'll tell you what Sammy this is probably as good a time as any to get over to India and track down my brother. I told you about him being over there before didn't I, I've just got to get my passport sorted and get a few things together, it's been long enough. I'll get down to Cambridge and get those postcards and things. He won't be hard to find. I'll just have to get the money together and get the passport sorted. Seems like a good opportunity. Most Sammy said all day was I'll tell you what Steve son my eyes are fucking killing me I can hardly see a fucking thing.

Other marks to body: no obvious signs of self-harm, no tattoos, no obvious evidence of injection sites. Visual appearance of body consistent with having remained in situ after death for a period of approximately seven days.

And what if they'd paid this much attention to us all. What if that therapist or whoever had laid Mike out on the table and said Tell me about this bruise here, and this scar, and this blister, and this, what's this, is this a cigarette burn? Are any of these the result of self-harm, Mike? It depends if you discount self-harm in the wider sense, like as in heroin addiction itself, as in like the associated

178

reckless disregard for one's own wellbeing. Because leaving that aside there is still cutting with blades and burning with cigarettes and there has been some of that yes. On account of the implants like. Having occasional reason to believe they've been misused as in recording certain facts and divulging them to certain agencies. You know what I mean. Burning can sometimes do the job but then sometimes he's had to go in with a blade and like carve the offending item right out. Didn't always get to it though pal. Sometimes it just goes deeper. The doctor or therapist going So these acts of self-harm aren't necessarily on a suicidal continuum. Mike looking at him. The bloke going Have you ever thought about suicide, Mike? I have my friend. I have. Usually when the voices get too bad and there don't seem like any other way of shutting them up. But also it would show people. That's what he thinks sometimes. It would teach them a lesson, there would have to be like an inquiry or something and it would show them how bad it was when they didn't believe him or didn't listen or didn't understand. It would show his family or like his friends from school if they even remembered. Or maybe it wouldn't show no one nothing like maybe they wouldn't even be riled.

Thought about doing it by deliberately going over, like most of the users he knows have thought about that, thinking about it half the time they shoot up. Thought about jumping, hanging, drowning, burning, walking into the wrong pub and getting himself stabbed. One thing he always came back to though was walking out in front of a bus. Kid at school done that and it had always stuck with him. Seemed like if you got it right it would be easy and quick and no one would ever know you'd done it on purpose, like if any of that God stuff turned out to be true like his parents said then you could maybe get away with it not looking too much like a mortal sin and all that.

He has thought about it. He has.

But all Robert's bruises don't count for much. Everyone's got them, after all. All of us. Bruises and the rest of it: cuts and grazes and sprains and breaks, abscesses and open infected sores. From digging, from falling, from walking into a fist or a bottle or a boot. Like Ben especially, short time we've known him he's more or less always had a black eye or something like it, his smart little mouth always earning him trouble but he never seems to mind. Always a big grin on when he takes the punch, laughing like Is that all you've got. Which usually gets him one more. Like Laura, second time she came back to her dad's we knew she was ready to stay around by the bruises she had. Up and down both arms and her fingernails weren't long or clean or polished no more. Never talked much about where she'd been but it didn't look like she'd gone back home to her mum's.

Said she'd gone off with some friends instead of going home. Spent the summer at some festivals, like climbing over fences and sleeping in other people's tents and selling pills to pay for food, and at the end of the summer she still didn't want to go home so she ended up living on a site for the winter. This was what she told Heather. What Heather tells us now, her voice hanging above us like smoke and lingering in the cold white room. She'd done the same round of festivals the next year, and ended up on another site for the winter, and basically got in to gear while she was staying there. It had been all right for a while but then it had all gone a bit dark so she'd sold her van and left the site. Come back up to her dad's to get herself sorted. Heather asked her if she meant sort of sorted clean or sorted sorted, and Laura said what did she think otherwise what would she be doing there?

The two of them in the front bedroom together, Laura's old room although she could hardly recognise it now, the two of them shooting up and sending someone out to score and shooting up again, and then Heather getting her started on the crack. She still had a wedge of money from selling the van, and the two of them soon binged their way through it. Heather showing her how to inject into her legs. Looking at her arms, stroking the blackening bruises and saying You've messed these up proper sweetheart you better leave them alone now. Pulling Laura's trousers down and kneeling on the floor beside her to find a good new vein, whispering sweetly while Laura brought it up and dug in the pin. Saying There you go love, that should do you nicely. Handing her a tissue to press on the spot where the needle had gone in before helping her pull up her trousers as she lay back down on the bed. Always made a point of leaning the door shut because she said she didn't think Robert should see but really she didn't want anyone to see. But we see now. The two of them lying on the bed together, touching each other's hair, nodding out for minutes and hours and then opening their eyes to talk. Laura saying How long you been doing this then, and Heather saying Too fucking long love but what does it matter. Laura saying Do you think my dad knows I'm using and Heather saying He might be pissed love but he's not stupid of course he knows. I think he's just happy to have you about the place. Which made Laura smile. Any parent would be, Heather said. Which made Laura smile even more. Resting the side of her face on her pressed-together hands, saying If my mum could see me now she'd go mental, she'd go totally get-out-of-my-house, that's why I came back here, I reckoned like my dad at least couldn't say much about it the state he's in. Looking at Heather's tattoo, the blue-green ink blurred by the ageing skin, pressing her fingers over it and saying Can you see me now? The two of them laughing. Heather saying The trouble that's got me into I reckon I should sue whoever done it. Like sort of loss of earnings. The two of them laughing, and all of us laughing now in this room at the thought of it, the sound of us still not quite making sense as we stand here around Robert's naked bloated body.

Remember the way Heather always laughed, a bit louder and a bit longer than everyone else, like it took her a while to get the joke and she had to make up for it.

Laura sliding on to the floor to get the works, already wriggling her trousers down and saying Heather do you want some more I want some more. Ben knocking on the door, moving it aside, looking down at Laura with her trousers around her knees and saying All right ladies I got your shopping. That grin on his face, spread right across his cheeks, his lips rolling round his teeth, trying not to look so pleased with himself, with his dark hair curling over his face and his hands reaching into his pockets to pull out the goods like a magic trick. Like some kind of showman, weren't he. How old was he then. Sixteen. Only just out of care, officially. Got himself out a long time before but he was still getting used to not looking over his shoulder all the time, to not worrying about getting caught and taken back. Was starting to miss it already in fact. The two of them reaching out and him teasing them for a moment, waving the gear above them, enjoying the passing thrill of power before dropping it into their outstretched hands. That was early on. When he would do missions for nothing, for fun and thanks and a bag or two he could keep to sell on himself. Was a lot of things he'd do for a word of thanks, then. The way it would light up his face.

Ben always had a lot to say but he never told us much. Always talking about going down to Brighton to find his sister. Said the last he'd heard she was staying down there, and if things didn't work out he could always go and track her down. Lost touch with her after she left care, she was supposed to come and visit but she didn't always make it. Didn't even get on with her that well, never had much to do with her after they got taken into care. But she's still his sister and that, she'd still help him out, probably. If he could get down to Brighton. If he could find her. She knows how it weren't his fault. She knows that's old news now. He couldn't have done nothing to stop him, to stop it happening. He didn't even know about it really, not enough to be sure. She took it out on Ben at the time but that's old news now, she wouldn't keep taking it out on him no more. If he could get down to Brighton. If he could find her. What would he have done anyway. He was only little. At the time when it happened. Anyway. Don't matter no more. Sweeping the hair out of his eyes. Bouncing up and down on his toes and looking all over, like he was getting ready to run. Always seemed like he was ready to run. Didn't he. Remember that. Don't you. Jesus.

The doctor moves over to the whiteboard and talks to his junior, asking if he's happy with their observations so far, if he has any further comments, and then he speaks to the woman with the black-rimmed glasses and says Okay, Jenny, I think it's time we had a proper look at our gentleman, could you do us the honour of opening him up? We see, through a window in one wall which looks on to a small office, the detective talking on his phone, drinking coffee from a poly-styrene cup and watching as Jenny takes a long scalpel from a steel tray of tools and slices into Robert's chest. There's a soft slow hissing sound as his chest and stomach deflate. The polished blade parts a long u-shaped line through his flesh, from one ear to his chest and then back to the other ear, the blood running in streams down each side of his body. She keeps cutting, and the blood keeps coming, thick and dark and draining away along the gullies in the sides of the table. She lifts the scalpel and makes another long cut, from the centre of the chest right down to the pubic bone, and then she peels back the flaps of tissue and skin, tugging them away from Robert's ribcage and laying them out flat on either side of his chest like the opened pages of a book. She peels away the third flap, at the top, draping it over Robert's face, and uses an electric saw to cut through each of his ribs. The noise of the saw fills the room, grinding and violent, and we step back for a moment. We turn away. This is difficult to watch, even now. How easily a body is reduced to this. Knotted sinew and fat and bone. Severed arteries and veins, the blood pouring out. The saw whines a little as it bites into each rib, the technician rocking on her toes as the blade breaks through the soft marrow and out the other side. She cuts through twelve ribs along his left side, stooping low over the table, and then circles round to cut through twelve more on the right. The saw whirrs to a noisy halt. The extraction fans in the table whistle softly as they suck the bone dust out of the air.

No obvious damage to ribcage, sternum or clavicle bones, the doctor says. No evidence of violence to the torso, nor of any attempted resuscitation.

Second time Laura came home she asked her dad if she could stay for a while. Remember that. He thought all his birthdays had come at once, thought he was going to keel over with it there and then. Thought things were going to be all right after that. He could see she'd got herself in a bit of trouble, bit of a mess, but it was something they had in common now, something they could get sorted out together, the two of them like a team, like father and daughter getting things right together, making up for lost time. Like fuck.

The pain in his head, sometimes. Blocking out everything Yvonne was saying to him, making him want her to go away, to be quiet, to just fucking shut up and go away that pain in his head like nothing else. But she didn't believe him, or she thought it was his drinking, or she thought he was being a wimp. Drinking was just about the only thing that made it go away. Like someone hammering a nail into the side of his head. Jesus what was it. If he kept moving he couldn't feel it. If he drank enough, and kept moving, and she shut up fucking shut up a minute it went away. But it always came back, and, sometimes. Made him act wrong sometimes.

The pain in his head when he first heard Yvonne warning him what she was going to do. The feel of the sound of it. Like a what, like a storm, like a storm behind glass. Shrieking into his face to make sure he could hear, beating on him. Her tight little fists shaking in the air. I'll go back to my mum's, I will. Are you listening to me. I don't want to but I can't stay here like this. And everything he'd heard her saying to her mum on the phone. No he hasn't been looking for a job yet but he, I thought he just needed a bit of time to get over it, it was such a shock the way they all got locked out like that with no warning, they all took it hard and it's not like they've had much help, I mean most of them just went straight on the sick. But he's had long enough now, it's been long enough, he could at least give me a hand about the place. Standing by the kitchen sink with another drink while she hid in the bedroom and said all this and she thought he couldn't hear. He's leaving everything down to me and I've had enough, there's bills stacking up, Mum, I've been swinging a few extra shifts but I still don't see how we're going to cover it all. I don't know, Mum. I don't know what I'm going to do. And Laura waking up to hear her mum shouting again, shouting I'll go back, Robert, I will, I'll take her with me and all, you bloody watch me, I don't want to but I will. Are you listening? Are you bloody well listening or what? And then the thumping, like before, coming through the wall, her mum's little fists against her dad's chest, pounding through him and the thin wall and knocking against Laura where she was sat up with her back against the headboard of her bed. Until it stopped, like it always did, and they were both crying, and she could hear the shuffling three-legged footsteps of the two of them helping each other to bed, and she fell asleep, and years later she was lying with her head in Heather's lap telling the story all over again. Not feeling nothing about it this time.

These things all coming together now. Coming up to the surface.

And remember Robert told Steve about it too. Said it had been more or less the only clue that something was up, that something was going wrong. Said he'd known she didn't like him drinking so much, and he'd known they'd been doing plenty of arguing, but he'd thought it was normal. But that's just it Rob mate, Steve told him, the two of them sitting in their armchairs in the empty room and working their way through the day's drinks, nothing's normal for them is it, nothing's good enough. They're always after things being different, being better. You're better off without mate, he said, and they knocked their cans together in agreement, looking out across the playing fields and the sun going down behind the trees by the river. That's what Steve told him. Didn't he. That's where he went wrong, he broke the golden rule, let himself get in too far. You start leaning on someone, when they do the off you'll fall over. Stands to reason. Never lean on no one. Never trust no bastard. Golden rule, that's what he told him. Remember that. That's where he went wrong with what's her name, as it happens, the woman from the shop. Marianna, Marianne, Marie. Whatever her name was. Let down his guard, got to the point where he'd do all sorts of bollocks for her, like he was trying to impress her, like he thought she was bothered. Then when he came back from that roadtrip to bloody Bosnia she didn't want to know. Said things had changed. Said Steve had changed, said he was too moody and it was too hard being around him any more. Too right he'd changed, what else did she expect. He'd seen a few things when he was over there. Things that had, even someone who'd been on all the postings he'd been on, they'd taken him aback a bit, more or less. He wasn't looking for sympathy, he'd never asked for that. Just a little bit of patience. A bit of understanding. She made out like he'd got too quiet and moody but she only

189

had to give him a chance to think. Just sometimes. Jesus. He was still up for a laugh and a joke but he needed to clear his head and she didn't really get it. Giving it all Maybe you should talk to someone about it, like that would help. There was that time, the two of them stood on the bridge over the canal, it was right when he was getting his tenancy sorted out and he'd said something about she could stay over sometimes and as soon as he'd said it he knew he was stuffed. She wouldn't even look at him. Hands deep in her pockets like she had a weapon hidden away in there. Giving it all Oh but the thing is really, Steve, things are a bit different now, things have got a bit weird. I wasn't really up for anything serious. Looking down at the muddy brown water like she was hoping he'd jump in or something. And after that the staff wouldn't let him work in the shop any more, or even go in there at all. They said it wasn't appropriate, which was a joke because he wasn't the one with the problem. He wasn't the one who'd said things had got a bit weird. He wouldn't have bloody minded only he never even got to bang her whatever her name was Maria or Marie or whatever. Would have liked to. She had nice hands and that.

The technician reaches across Robert, grasping the top of his ribcage and lifting it away from his body. It comes off in one piece, like the breast-plate from a suit of armour, and she lays it down

190

on another stainless-steel table. We move in close around his body again, our hands resting on the table, and peer in at the strange swollen gleam of his insides, the flabby organs crammed wetly in upon each other. The doctor scrapes away more layers of creamy yellow fat, slices through a series of arteries and veins, and then lifts the organs out as a single block, easing them on to a plastic tray which they carry over to a cutting board on the counter running along the wall. Behind them, in the scooped-out hollow of Robert's body, we see the rib-bones fanning out across his back, the knuckles of his spine, the coiled mass of his intestines and bowels already slipping and spreading out to fill the space.

Should be something more like. We prop photos up amongst the candles, snapshots from younger days, better days, so that people can look and tell lies about how he hasn't aged all that badly, considering. A photo from his army days, in full dress uniform, so that his former colleagues can pick it up and put it down and catch each other's eyes and not need to say a word. A photo Laura once found in the bottom of her mum's wardrobe, of a young-looking man with a soft round face and a broad flat chest, his shirt hanging open and a young girl grinning wildly on his shoulders. She used to go and look at it when her mum was out of the house. The young girl on the shoulders was her, she supposed.

191

All those years thinking about him, and once she was back there she found it hard to think of him as her dad at all. He didn't even look much like that photo, by the time she got to him. The Robert she met – fat with drink and sorrow, unwashed, with a crushed face and a sunken posture, each hand punched into an arthritic curl – was the man her mother had warned her about, the man she'd always been told they'd left. The man Robert had only really become once they'd closed that door behind them and he'd started drinking seriously. Once he'd given up expecting them to ever come home. She'd imagined hugging him when she came back. Sitting on his lap, resting her head on his shoulder. Making up for everything they'd lost. Which had sort of happened, once, soon after the second time she came back, putting her arms around him and clinging on desperately until the smell of his long-worn clothes had pushed her away. After that, she'd only ever touched him when she wanted money. Crouching beside him and resting a hand on his knee, or standing behind him with her hands on his shoulders, leaning over and talking softly into his ear. She felt bad asking, but she felt like he owed her. All those years he hadn't been around. That one time though, she thought about it sometimes. When she wasn't thinking about other things. The way it felt. Nothing like she'd been expecting. The solid, numbed stillness of him. Like hugging a tree. His arms by his side, lifting out into the air for a moment, uncertainly. Like he'd forgotten what he was supposed to do, and by the time he'd remembered she'd already gone, again.

They stand around the cutting board, the doctor and the technician and the assistants and the photographer. The rest of us pressing in around them. The doctor separates out the liver, lifting it in one hand and resting it in the shining bowl of an electronic set of scales. Two thousand seven hundred and forty-three grammes, he says, and one of them just about whistles, and the junior doctor writes it down on the whiteboard. The liver is a yellowish orange colour, like a sponge, speckled and grainy, and thick gobbets of fat spread out across the knife as the doctor slices into it. What can you tell me about this? he asks his junior. Cirrhosis, the younger man says. Advanced cirrhosis. Thank you, the doctor says, smiling. The technician takes one of the liver slices and puts it into a clear plastic container, soaking it with formaldehyde and carefully labelling the lid. The doctor separates out the heart, an awkward-looking lump of flesh with severed pipes and tubes fingering out in all directions, weighs it, and puts it back on the board. He cuts into it, exposing the chambers, the valves, the arteries, using his scalpel to indicate particular features while he dictates his notes.

Heart: enlarged, flabby, otherwise of normal external appearance, firm, reddish brown, no lesions apparent. Left and right ventricles normal, cardiac chambers normal although some clotted blood apparent, endocardium normal. Sections through the coronary arteries show significant narrowing, of approximately seventy to eighty per cent, indicating severe coronary artery disease.

If it comes down to it la I will cut out your heart.

Remember Danny and Laura and Heather and Ben all cooking up together one time. Down under one of the arches by the canal because Mike was up at the flat and he hadn't put any money in for the gear. Was it that or just we didn't want him around. Danny doing all the prep and the rest of them watching like coppers so the shares would be even. Got a couple of two and one deals between them all, so he mixed up the dark and the light in the spoon and got it cooking, drew the whole lot up into one barrel to measure it and then squirted it back out into the spoon, shared it out into everyone's pins, and then everyone backed off to get digging. Heather laughing at Ben because he said he still didn't like needles and that was a fucking joke that made them laugh every time. Danny and Laura going at the same time, bang on the same time, the crack kicking in first and the two of them watching each other when it did, some kind of fucking beautiful going off there between them for what is it seconds a minute two minutes like you you euphoric between them like a whoosh like a bullet through a tunnel bursting out

194

into the sunshine firelight with this what this great big God almighty yes yes yes before sinking settling down into the cotton-wool embrace of the dark the brown taking the edge off taking the edge all the way right fucking off. Heather still laughing away at Ben, going I reckon you're in the wrong fucking line of work here Benny boy, all four of them laughing and lying back on to the rubble and ash under the arch, listening to the white-noise roar of the water pouring over the top of the lock, the clatter of the trains running over them, Danny turning to look in Laura's eyes again but she was all gone away. Rubbing his fingers over and over his face, feeling well, feeling welcome in his body again. Feeling like, fuck, the things a body can do, these fingers, these bones, this muscle and skin, the bones of his face, the jaw and the cheeks and the eye sockets, the cells dividing and forming and healing and beginning again, all the things we do to these bodies and they keep beginning again, the cuts and bruises and festering wounds, this crash helmet of a skull keeping this suffering brain safe. For what. For this. For this feeling well again. For all the things a body can be. For when all this is over and done with and life can begin again.

Would like to have seen her naked one time. Just once. Probably she was all fucked up, all bones and bruises and broken veins, but still even so. Would have liked to see what her body could do, what her body could be. Long and white and pale and turning towards. Opening towards.

And what about Ben. Jesus. That time in Laura's old bedroom when Heather had some rocks to offer him. No one really knew about it at the time except we knew something had gone off. We know about it now though but. Pulling him into the room and closing the door. Sitting down on the bed, near enough falling down on the bed, saying Come here Benny boy do you want a smoke do you want a go on the pipe? Reaching in her pocket and taking out a bag. Ben smiling that smile again and going Heather mate does the Pope shit in the woods or what? Heather filling a pipe for him and offering it up, and Ben's brain going pop pop pop as he sucked away on it. Heather waiting, watching, Ben chatting on about the trouble he'd been having at the hostel, something to do with another resident lying to the staff about him tooting in his room and when the staff came to search it they planted some rocks under the mattress because they had it in for him anyway they wanted an excuse to get him out of there he'd been lippy one time too many and they like you to know who's in charge who's the boss who's the fucking what what the number one. Heather watching his eyes flicker to the pipe and the lighter and the bag hidden tightly in her fist. Ben stuttering and stopping and saying Heather I'm not being cheeky or nothing but can I have some more? The hunger it gives you, the need. Nothing you could ever need as much as another go on the pipe. The first time the best time and you're always chasing after that. Do anything to get back to that. Never get there but you always get close and you always keep reaching. Don't you. Heather looking up at him, her eyes unfouced, saying Come here then. Lowering her voice and saying Come here. Putting her hands out and pulling him towards her by the waistband of his jeans. Ben pulling away, and Heather pulling him back, saying Come here Ben, come here, pulling him to the edge of the bed and keeping him there with her legs squashed around his. Looking at him looking at the pipe. Looking at him as she undoes his trousers and keeps him from pulling away. Saying Come on Ben, come on. What are you scared of? You've known me long enough, haven't you? Come on, come on. It's not going to do any harm. Ben looking away, to the battered wall behind the bed, to the corner of the room, saying Heather I don't really want to. I don't want. Heather still murmuring, reassuring, one hand behind him now and the other hand working on him through his pants. Saying Do me a favour love. If you want another go on the pipe. There's plenty more where the last lot came from. Saying What's the matter Ben, don't you like me or something? And Ben, his whole body stiffened and still, saying Heather it's not that of course I like you it's just it's not like that I don't want to. Cold resignation in his voice. Taking the pipe as she hands it up to him. Taking long blistering draws on the smoke while she pulls down his pants and does what she wants to do, squeezing his balls, tugging at his unwilling erection, working her calloused fingers into the crack of his arse while a smell like pear drops bubbles into the room and his brain goes pop pop pop and he pictures the light sparkling round through his bloodstream, surging, charging, roaring, picking him up up up and over the room looking down and further right out of the room and the first time he met Heather outside the train station where he was tapping people up and she told him You don't want to do that here sweetheart you'll get picked up in no time, couple of coppers on the way over even while she was talking and she took his arm and led him straight off down the road. Weight of her hand on his elbow. Her wide round hips squashing into his. Funny-looking woman but he didn't mind going off with her, seemed like she knew a thing or two. Leading him like a blind man which is what he was more or less when it came to living out on the street. Was a lot better now but he never saw this one coming. Should have done but he didn't, the pipe burning dry and the popping in his brain fading away and the anxious gnawing appetite sliding back in. Looking down at the back of her head while she sucks away at him, her greasy half-red hair with the black roots turning grey, the smell of the burning crack drifting off and the smell of her replacing it, the smell of drink and old sweat and bad teeth and he tries to pull her head away by the hair but she don't stop. Saying

198

Fucking stop it stop it Heather will you stop it please. Things she warned him about but she never warned him about this. Heather wiping her mouth and smiling and saying Oh come on Benny boy, what's wrong, you don't want any more goes on the pipe? Looking at him looking at the bag of rocks in her fist. Saying Come on now Ben. No one's going to know. I won't tell anyone. Come on. Give me some more and I'll give you what you need. Her hands all over in between his legs now, pulling at him, pinching and scratching him and pulling him closer. Ben turning his face towards the ceiling and screwing up his eyes. Saying Heather fucking hell fucksake. Saying it under his breath as if daring himself to say it, fucking hell Heather I don't want to. You stupid fucking bitch. Heather's eyes widening with anticipation when he says this, wrestling with her own trousers, the belt and the buttons and the tangle of shirts and shawls hanging around them, kicking the trousers to her ankles and falling back on to the bed. Pulling Ben down on to her and tugging him in and saying Say that again. Say bitch again. Ben with his eyes screwed shut but still the smell of her all over and the soft rolling slap of her body beneath him and the grunt and moan of her gaping crack-headed need swallowing him up. Thought he could trust her even though one thing she warned him was never trust no one and it turns out she was right about that. Should have learnt it years ago but. Way back when all those people

199

he thought were helping him out were just grassing him up and getting him sent back to the home. In the day centre. At the church. That woman at the train station when he tried to jump the barriers. That bloke he asked for money outside the theatre who put him up for the night. All of them going Yeah yeah I'll help you out, son, and then running off to phone up and get him shipped off back to the home. Too late for them now though. They couldn't do that no more, he was too old for care, too old to get taken back, he was on his own now and he liked it that way, it was better that way. Old enough to look after himself and he had been for a long time. Heather going Hold me down then now, like a bastard, you're a bastard, go on, hold my wrists. Ben opening his eyes for a second and saying Fucksake Heather you mad fucking bitch, bitch, bitch, you mad fucking bitch, saying it to a rhythm without even meaning to and then holding her wrists down on the bed, thinking about the pipe, trying to think about nothing but the pipe and feeling himself lifted high above the room but still hearing her and feeling her and smelling her even with his eyes screwed tightly shut, the scabs and bruises of her thighs clenched around his legs, the cigarette burns across her stomach, her grunting and moaning and going Pull my hair fucking pull my hair you bastard you bastard and Ben trying not to listen, trying not to think of nothing but the pipe at the end of all this going You fat, fucking, bitch, you sick, fat, fucking, bitch, you sick, fucking, fucking, fucking, and Heather going Yes yes no please no.

We didn't know this, before. Even Heather says she didn't know, she sort of can't remember, she must have been sort of out of it and she can't quite believe it was her. But we know it now, we see it and we believe it now. None of us is shocked. Most of us have known something like it before anyhow. None of this is new. None of it matters no more.

The doctor turns back to the board and cuts open Robert's lungs, and the airways spill into his hands like roots pulled up from the soil.

Lungs: normal external colour and appearance, heavy. Airways congested with aspirated blood. Primary bronchi and successive bronchi showing signs of tar-like deposits probably from cigarette smoke. Dilated airspaces at extreme upper lobes indicate probable emphysema. Note that trachea and large airways also contain blood.

The technician puts the heart and lungs and liver into a red plastic bag, and the photographer takes more pictures as the doctor weighs and dissects the other organs on the board. He shows something to the others, gesturing with his scalpel, and the technician goes to Robert's hollowed body and fetches short lengths of his intestines, snipping them loose with a pair of blunt-nosed scissors and carrying them over to the workbench. She slices them open, washes them out at the sink, and puts them to one side. The doctor speaks again, and his junior makes more notes on the whiteboard.

Stomach: normal external appearance and colour, compressed and empty of food contents. Small intestine also empty of digestive content; descending section of large intestine contains faecal matter; conclude that the deceased had not consumed food for a period of approximately twenty-four to forty-eight hours prior to death.

We sit around talking in low voices, looking at him, and someone puts on his favourite CD, Neil Young singing I'm going to give you till the morning comes, and someone else comes out the kitchen with plates of sandwiches, sliced ham and cucumber and cottage cheese. Cut into little triangles and passed around the room, and when someone says Oh I couldn't possibly someone else says Eh now come on you'll want to keep your strength up la. And we light more candles. Do we bollocks.

People think it's all about being hungry and that but hungry's got nothing to do with it. Can always find food if you want it. Soup runs and day centres and hostels and that. Food don't cost much. Food don't cost nothing if you know where to look. Can go without eating for a couple of days, more when there's other stuff you need to sort first. Like getting sorted. Food don't matter when you got the rattles coming on, and when you're sorted you don't even care. But Robert always liked his food didn't he though. Was always after sending someone out to get him something. Pizzas and kebabs and all that. Don't know where he got the money from but he was never short of food. Something must have happened if he didn't eat nothing for twenty-four hours. Something must have gone off. All that talk about where he got the money from but he never went short of food or drink. These little shits tried robbing him once but they only found a tenner on him. Remember that. They never tried it again after we'd done with them. Must have kept it somewhere but. Liked having something to eat.

Little shits must have been waiting for us all to go out, watching, because they got Robert when he was on his own and we didn't often leave him on his own. Said he liked company. He gave them what they could find, a tenner and some fags and a bottle of cider, and he got a good look at their faces while they were knocking him about, and as soon as we got back he told us who it was. We didn't need telling twice though did we. Remember that. That was what it was, it was like a what, an unspoken deal. He let us hang out in his flat, do what we wanted there more or less, sleep there if we needed to, and we looked out for him. Got rid of people he didn't want there. Sorted out his debts. And found the little shits who tried to tax him, followed them down to the underpass near the canal and near enough broke their fucking legs with a short bit of scaffold pole that Ben had happened to find along the way. Only two of them so it weren't hard. Certain things we'd all do for Robert and that was one of them.

He shouldn't be here. We shouldn't be here. He should be in some fucking what some funeral home or something all laid out nice with flowers and candles and what and music. We should be here to pay our respects instead of all this. Who's going to lay him out now. Where will they take him. The state of him once this lot have done. The box they'll have to cart him off in, and who's going to stick him in the ground, who's going to pay for all that. No one's going to get Yvonne to come back. Not now, not when she's so far away. His parents are long gone. And will they find Laura, does anyone even know who she is. Someone's got to take him and bury him and say all the prayers and all that. He shouldn't be here, he shouldn't even fucking be here. We shouldn't be here.

Always in the wrong place, the wrong time. The wrong fucking body, the wrong fucking skin.

And remember what Laura said that time, about wanting a new body, wanting to start again with a new body so she could go round all over again. Don't work like that but she wanted it to. When Danny found her that time. When she'd run out of veins or she thought she had. Been trying to get a dig for over an hour, sitting there by herself just poking around with the pin trying to get in to all those collapsed and raggedy veins, trying to find the other ones deeper in but the pin weren't long enough. Rooting around and getting more and more desperate, more and more scared. Danny found her round by the bins behind the hostel and for a minute he thought she'd been cutting herself. All that blood. Looked like it was just seeping out through her skin. She was crying and swearing and going Danny fucking what Danny what am I going to do now? Scratching her neck and pulling her hair and going Danny I've been trying for fucking ages I can't do it. What the fuck have I done? Cold and white and the rattles on her so bad he could more or less hear them. Blood all over her hands, and then blood all over Danny's hands when he tried to find a dig for her. Her voice all thin and tired going Danny fucking what what I need to fucking start all over again or something don't I. Don't even want to stop but maybe I got no choice. Danny giving up in the end and finding Mike, Mike coming round and sticking one in her neck, going You don't wanna try this yoursen though la, you need to see what you're doing an it's too easy to pop an artery, you know what I'm saying. It's game over when you do that an no mistake. Laura with her chin right up looking way past Mike to the sky, her eyes spilling with tears and holding her breath while he eased in the pin. Clinging on to his arms to keep still, like he was her only hope or something. Like he was the one who could make her body new. A new body and what though but. A new heaven and all that. All Laura wanted was one more vein. One more chance to begin again.

Ben had a laugh when she said that. No chance of that is there, no one gets a second go and anyone who says you do is talking fucking bollocks. Laughing like it was a joke but he weren't joking. Was he. Sweeping the hair out of his eyes and sniffing and smearing the snot from his nose with the back of his hand. No one gets a second go. Where was it. Remember that. Where were we when. Climbing up the garages round the back of Robert's flat to get in that time, after he couldn't get to the front door to open it. Mike giving Danny a leg up and Benny boy talking to Laura while they waited their turn and Einstein sniffing around the garage doors. Only a few days after Mike had helped her do the vein in her neck and she was talking about wanting another chance. Maybe if I give it a rest I can start up again once it's healed, she said. The old woman with the tiger-paw slippers walking her dog round the edge of the playing fields and giving them a funny look like they were up to something. Her and her rat-faced little Yorkshire terrier with the tartan jacket, and Mike telling her she could take a picture if she wanted and that sent her shuffling on her way. When was this. Laura said What you talking about second goes and that, what would you know, you're not

206

even old enough to have had a first go yet. I don't know about that Laura, he said, smiling even more than usual, I'm old enough, I'm old enough for a bit of you know what. She laughed, and reached out to smack him round the head, and as he ducked out of reach he grabbed her wrist and said Don't you dare don't you fucking dare. Pulling his face close to hers and stopping himself from saying whatever he was going to say next, pulling his face close enough that their foreheads touched, until she pulled away and told him to fuck off. The two of them out of breath a little, and the old woman watching them again, and Mike and Danny out of sight on the garage roof. And that smile again, and Ben going No but leave it out will you I don't like girls giving out like that, it's not right. What was he talking about. What did he mean. How should we know. Mike leaning over the edge of the roof and reaching out his hand, going Up you come la there's room for everyone, up you come the two of youse. And then climbing in through that kitchen window and Robert sitting in his chair laughing at them all, that laugh deep down in his belly going Here comes the cavalry! Here comes the fucking mountain rescue! What you got for you Uncle Robert? When was this. Three days before Christmas. So what happened then.

This was the same day Laura got Danny in her room for that one last hit. Which her worker had warned her about hadn't he. Giving it all It's so important that you stick to your script, Laura, you need to be clean when you start rehab, there's no such thing as one last go, it doesn't work like that, you know it doesn't work like that. So then she was all panicking and crying and everything. After she'd kicked Danny out and after she came down off her nod she was all in a panic because she thought she'd fucked it all up again. Trying to phone her worker and explain and they kept going He's out of the office now. Getting the hostel staff to find him, asking them to call the rehab and sort something out. Asking them to help her now. Thinking she'd blown her only chance and when she managed to speak to her worker the first thing he said was Listen, Laura, there's always another chance. But let's try and make this one work. And he must have made some calls because next thing was she was sat in the room with him and one of the hostel staff, what was her name, Ruth or someone, and he's going Okay here's the plan. They're still going to take you, and they're going to take you early, you can go up there tomorrow, they'll put you on a detox before you start the course. And until then the best thing you can do is stay in your room, watch the television, don't talk to anyone, don't answer the door. Ruth's going to bring you up some food, and she's going to look after your mobile, and you're going to sit tight until a taxi comes for you tomorrow. Do you think you can manage that? Laura crying and everything and nodding yes and then what.

Climbed in the taxi with a couple of bags of clothes and drove out of town to the rehab, to the house in the country with the tall trees and the long sloping lawn. Into the, fucking, sunset and that. Easy as that. Stopped at Robert's on the way, said her goodbyes and whatever else. And what else.

The doctor turns away from the cutting board and says Jenny, I think we'll move on shall we? Jenny nods, and moves back to Robert's body, to his head. She takes a new scalpel from the tray of polished tools and slices a long line across Robert's scalp, slipping through the matted black hair and the raw reddened skin and the thin layer of flesh, the tip of the blade scraping against his skull. She takes the incision right across the crown, from ear to ear, and then peels back each segment of scalp like the skin of a bloody orange. She picks up the electric saw, and leans forward to brace her feet, and cuts a circle around Robert's skull, the growl and grind of the saw once again filling the room. She puts the saw to one side, and she lifts off the top of Robert's head.

We look at his brain, Robert's brain, creamy-white and glistening, soft and heavy, fold upon fold of interconnected flesh which once fizzed with electrical code, with memories and visions and language and everything learnt in his short and thwarted life. We look at the doctor's fingers moving around it, squeezing, prodding, tracing lines and shapes as he talks to the others, making comments, asking questions. We watch his fingers catch on something as he pushes down into the skull, and we watch him delicately work loose a dull-coloured fragment of metal the size of a fifty-pence piece. He holds it up to the light, and the photographer takes pictures, and they pass it between them, turning it over and over in their gloved palms. The doctor combs through Robert's hair, above his ear, behind his ear, further round to the nape of his neck, and finds a faded scar, crescent-shaped, slightly ridged, about the length of a fifty-pence piece. The detective knocks on the window, and we hear his voice coming through a speaker overhead. Something interesting? he asks. I don't know, the doctor says. Looks like it might be shrapnel of some kind. Looks old though. How old? the detective asks. Too old for you, the doctor says, and the detective goes back to his newspaper. The technician takes a long-bladed knife and slips it down into the skull to slice through the top of the spinal column. She takes Robert's brain out of his head, places it in a plastic tray, and carries it over to the cutting board, where they weigh it and measure it and slice off samples to be stored in small plastic containers for further examination. The technician's assistant places the fragment of metal into a plastic pouch, and the doctor dictates more notes.

Brain: normal appearance, softened by decomposition. No evidence of haemorrhage. Brown discoloration and glial scarring to small area of the surface around the lower midpoint of the left cerebral hemisphere, this appears to have been caused by the ingress and or the remaining presence of a metallic fragment whose composition and origin is unknown. Fragment sent for analysis. Medical records of subject, once identified, may provide further information. Fragment appears to correspond with a scar around the left side of the base of the subject's skull, immediately above the hairline; possibility that this marks the original entry wound for fragment.

He backs away from the brain on the board, peeling off his outer layer of gloves and moving over to the whiteboard. He looks at the notes which have been written up, and asks his junior for any further comments. The detective's voice comes out of the overhead speaker again, saying We're done then are we? and the doctor says Sorry, Chris, there's nothing criminal here. Not unless the toxicology comes back and it turns out your gentleman's been poisoned by arsenic. In which case it'll probably be the butler what done it. Jenny finishes labelling all the sliced samples of Robert's organs and tissue and blood, slipping them into labelled plastic bags marked with biohazard stickers. She puts the slices of his brain into a red plastic bag lying open beside her. She packs cotton wadding into the scooped cavity of his skull, positioning the skull cap over it and pressing the two peeled-back flaps of scalp into place. She takes a needle and thread from the tray and stitches the scalp back together, stooping closely over it, taking her time. When she's finished she carefully brushes Robert's hair across the dotted threads, and as she stands back his head looks almost untouched. She smooths a stray hair back into place. She goes back to the cutting board, and places the rest of Robert's organs in the red plastic bag with his brain. She puts the intestines and bowels into another bag, and nestles them both into the bare-ribbed cavity of Robert's chest. She takes the sawn-off section of ribcage from the table and settles it back into place, and she folds the fatty flaps of flesh and skin back down together, picking up the needle and thread and stitching his body shut, working slowly and patiently while the others talk by the whiteboard, and when she's finished there's only a delicate Y-shaped seam to show he's been cut apart at all.

Someone else comes in, and we move closer to the table where he lies. We light more candles, rest our hands upon his body, and wonder what more we can say. Someone asks about the funeral arrangements. Mike says Eh now there's something you should see. I think youse had all best come and look at this. We look at each other, and we stand and follow him out through the door, out into the cold cracked dawn, walking along the empty streets and looking into alleyways and open garages, railway arches, tunnels, derelict buildings, the backyards of offices and pubs, the basements of multi-storey carparks, the locked rooms of hostels, the squatted flats above shops, the wasteground by the Miller's Arms. And Mike says, There you go, there's Danny. Slumped on the piss-wet floor of the phonebox. Einstein barking and yelping and hurling herself against the door. The bloody pin still in his hand, and his lips turning white, and his fingers folding over into claws. Curled up on the floor of the phonebox like a dog in a basket. Going over. Which we've all come close to doing before. Come close to that edge which is like no edge at all just a falling away of the ground. Always trying to get close to that, back to that peaceful place. To that, fucking, heaven. To be lifted, and held. Keep taking more and more to get back to that, to get past just feeling well again and all the way back to that peaceful place, and the more and more only takes us closer to going over. Which is like. What. Like, fucking, what was it, take the best orgasm you've ever had and multiply it by a hundred. And multiply it by a hundred again, and again, and it don't stop, and you keep coming and coming until you can't breathe, you can't think, you can't see or feel or hear nothing and your life goes pounding out of you in these great awful ecstatic thumps. And like, fucking, you're still nowhere near.

And Mike says Eh keep up now I got some other place to be. And we follow him back down the hill. Past the Parkside flats and under the motorway bridge to the canal, across the lockgates and along the towpath and over a brick wall and up to a flat above a boarded-up shop. And we see Steve. Laid out on the mattress in his tidy, whitewashed room. His bare feet pointing to the ceiling. His boots placed neatly side by side, and his socks laid out to dry. One arm folded over his chest, the other arm hanging off the side of the mattress, his once filthy hand licked clean. H lying on the floor with his head on his front paws, waiting.

And we see Ant. Stretched out on the floor nearby, his works arranged carefully on a square of black cloth between them. His body stiffening and slackening again even while we watch. The flies already arriving to lay their eggs, in his mouth, in his eyes, in the weeping needle holes up and down his arms.

And Mike strides off again, turning to beckon us on and muttering Will you come on now then will you, and we follow him further along the canal, past the arches, up to the train station and the bus station and the multi-storey carpark where we clatter down the concrete stairs to the base-ment. Did you think there would be answers. Did you think there would be reasons given. We hurry along the rippled concrete floor, past the glass-walled booth where the staff take their breaks and watch the cctv, down to the far end and the goods lift and the heavy-wheeled bins. Did you think anyone would know all these things or be able to explain. And Mike stands there and waits and then we see Ben. Curled up on the floor like he's just gone to sleep. Like he's tried to put himself in the recovery position but not quite managed. A puddle of sick beside his stone-cold face. The empty pin flung away. This is all just a coincidence, is it. All these. In this short little span of time. Come looking for reasons if you want but there's nothing to it. This was always going to happen some time and it don't mean nothing now.

And we keep walking through the empty streets, and we get to another whitewashed room where no guests are allowed, with the long white curtains blowing in across the bed and a carrier bag of shopping on the floor. We stand in the kitchen area at one end of the room, and we see another bag of shopping on the worktop. Toast crumbs spread across a board. A postcard and a magazine. A cold cup of tea, the surface bubbling with mould while we watch. And we see Heather and we turn away. The rot set in and the awful smell of death. Kneeling stiff by the side of the bed, her face sinking into the mattress. Her hands, black with blood, hanging heavy by her sides. That's everyone then, is it. That's all of us accounted for.

And Mike says Eh now then la I'll be off. I got some things I need to do. I got a bus to catch. And we turn and watch, and we see Mike, still talking into his phone, his long coat flapping around his knees, striding out into the middle of the road. We see the bus coming, slowing but not stopping and Mike turning with his arms outstretched going I feel much better now thanks. The look on the driver's face. We see an ambulance, and a police car, and a hospital bed. We see Mike going Eh now pal will you come and look at this, will you come and see the things I've seen. Got a bus to catch. Couldn't even get that right.

They wash him again, and comb his hair, and slide him on to a long metal trolley. They cover his body with a thin cotton shroud, tying it at the neck and the wrists, and they wrap him in a long white sheet. They wheel him back into the other room, and put him away behind one of the heavy steel doors. They sign more forms. The technician's assistant takes the trolley of bagged and packaged samples – slices of Robert's brain, heart, liver, kidney and lungs, the clippings of his hair and nails, vials of his blackened blood – and pushes it out along the corridor to a table by a hatch in the wall, to be collected and sent on to the labs. And then they all disrobe, peeling off their gloves and sleeve protectors and aprons and scrubbing their hands for a long time at the deep stainless-steel sinks. They go to the shower rooms next door, and we hear the pound of steaming water, shouted conversations, the flap of clean white towels. And while the others are still getting dressed, the doctor comes out into his office and begins to write up his notes. We look over his shoulder, but we have trouble reading his writing, and trouble understanding what we can read. He looks up through the window at the comments on the whiteboard, and carries on filling in forms. We look through the window at the empty steel table, clean again now, with its coiled hose and drainage channels and silenced extraction fans. The doctor stops writing, and puts away the file, and goes upstairs to join the others for lunch.

We wait, days and weeks in that lifeless room with Robert behind the heavy steel door. The reports come back form the labs, and we stand over the doctor while he fills out the blanks in his reports. We should go now. There should be something more we can do. We hear more footsteps in the long corridor outside. Keys, voices, the door being unlocked. They open the steel door and slide Robert out on to another trolley, folding back the white cloth so that only his face can be seen. They wheel him into another room. We go with them. The lights are turned low. There are thick curtains, and comfortable chairs against one wall, and a box of tissues beside the chairs. They lay a heavy embroidered cloth across his body. It hangs down and touches the floor. What is this. They step outside, and step back in, and we see Laura, and a policeman, the younger policeman from the flat. They stand at the far side of the room, talking. And Laura comes forward, and we move aside to let them pass. Is she ready for this. She sees him and she stops and she moves closer and she looks and she nods and says something. She says something to the policeman and he thanks her and steps back. We all step away. We leave Laura there beside him. She looks at his cold blank face. She glances along the length of his body. She reaches out her hands, and they hover above him. She says something. She lifts a hand and holds it in the air and she says something. One of the men standing by the door glances at the policeman and gestures with his eyes. The policeman moves forward and touches her arm and she turns away. And then they're gone, the door closing behind them with a quiet click. And Robert lies alone on the trolley, the room echoing with the small movements of her hands, her staggered breaths, the whisper of her voice saying Yes, that's him.

CHAPTER 5

They carry his body to the edge of town and throw him into the fire.

What do we do now.

We go with them and we stay with Robert and when someone fetches the doctor's report we follow to see where they go. And we come to an empty room. Push our way in and sit at the back. What is this place. Long and narrow. Rows of soft blue chairs. A raised platform at the other end of the room with a panelled desk and a heavy carved chair and some coat of arms like a lion and unicorn. A table on one side with a tape machine and a pad of paper. A large wilting spider plant and some spare chairs in the corner. Another table in front of the platform with another pad of paper and a box of tissues. One tissue sticking out ready. A clock on the wall behind us. We shift on our seats. Someone comes in through a door at one side with a jug of water and some plastic beakers and a stack of papers. She arranges the jug and the beakers on the table with the tape machine and she lays the papers out across the panelled desk. Light pours in through the arched windows down one side of the room. Striped by the slanting blinds. Buses rattle past along the main road outside. We hear voices and the door opens and the same woman comes back with the policeman who first found Robert. She shows him where to sit and she leaves. He looks around. He holds a notebook in his lap and crosses his legs. The door opens again and the woman comes in with Laura and shows her where to sit. And she says All rise for the coroner, will the court please rise.

CORONER: Thank you. Please be seated.

Before beginning this morning, I'd like to give you some explanation of the inquest process, and of my role as coroner.

This is not a criminal court: no one is on trial today, and no one will be found to be nor accused of being responsible for Mr Robert Radcliffe's death.

We are here to investigate the facts, and to record them, and to answer four questions which I am legally required to ask: who the deceased person was, where he came by his death, when he came by his death, and how he came by his death. The answers to these questions will constitute the verdict of this inquest. In the course of reaching that verdict I shall be asking witnesses to come to the stand and answer any questions I may have about the circumstances surrounding Mr Radcliffe's death. The law also allows me to invite what are known as Properly Interested Persons to ask their own questions of those witnesses, should they so wish. For our purposes today Laura Radcliffe will be recognised, as a relative of the deceased, as a Properly Interested Person.

Are there any questions at this stage?

What do we do now. Where do we go. Did any of us think it would be like this. When we started. When Laura started did she think this would. Did she think it would end up here. When she started. When she would try anything. What was it. When she thought she could do anything just to prove that her mum and Paul couldn't say. When they said We've got your best intentions at heart. And all that. But what was it was it that. Takes more than that. Easy to find blame some place but it don't mean nothing now.

CORONER: . . . is to ensure that the deceased person is granted a full and open hearing of the facts in a public manner. You may note the absence of journalists or members of the public in court this morning; nevertheless, this is a public court, and what we say here today will be a matter of public record. [Could I just ask, Ms Radcliffe: do you have any objection to me calling you Laura? (*Inaudible response.*) Thank you.]

We have a responsibility towards the deceased, and I trust that as his daughter, Laura, you will feel that we at the coroner's court are doing our utmost to uphold that.

I might also add, of course, that whilst we are here to perform an important task we are doing so in the context of the sadness of Mr Radcliffe's death, and I would like to extend the sympathies of the court to you, Laura, and to thank you for being here at what I know must be a difficult and distressing time.

What do we do now. Where do we go. We sit at the back of the court and we listen to everything they say. We sit in the cold dark room and we wait until someone comes back for his body. They will come back. They have to. Someone has to do something with him now. Take him away. Now they know. We read the reports and we look at the notes and the photographs and we read the transcript of the inquest tucked away in the files. We sit and we look at Laura. In the court. In the front row of these soft blue chairs. Sitting with her hands pressed into her lap, leaning forward to look at the judge. Coroner, judge, whatever. We hear more footsteps in the long corridor outside. Voices. Keys. The door being unlocked. A long metal trolley is pushed into the room and the men who drove the darkened van away from Robert's flat come to take him away again. Rolling him out from behind the heavy doors and sliding him on to the trolley and signing more forms before they push him out down the corridor to the shuttered doorway and the new day's sunlight pouring in down the long concrete ramp. We go with them. What else can we do.

CORONER: . . . on to the first of our four questions: who has died? I quote here from a report prepared by one of my officers.

The identity of the deceased was not immediately apparent upon the discovery of the body: although he was found in his own flat, there was nothing to confirm that he was the listed tenant, nor were any identifying documents found on his body. A number of papers were found in an envelope under the mattress in one of the bedrooms, principally documents connected with the claiming of benefits; however, as they were in more than one person's name they were of little immediate value.

The next-door neighbour said that she didn't know any of the names of the people who lived or congregated at the flat, and declined to identify the body. The council housing department stated that the flat was unoccupied and awaiting repairs, the last tenant having been evicted some years previously. The name of this supposedly evicted tenant matched the name on one of the benefits claims documents which had been found in the flat, that of Robert John Radcliffe.

At this point my officers sought the dental records of said Robert Radcliffe, which proved to be unobtainable. Meanwhile, a matching set of fingerprints had been found on the criminal records database, but under another name; a name similar but not identical to another of the names on the benefits claims forms found in the flat.

It was beginning to appear that whilst dying without an identity in a modern bureaucratic country such as ours is exceedingly difficult, dying with multiple identities is all too easy, and equally problematic.

However, further enquiries did eventually lead us to make contact with Laura Radcliffe, who was at that time attending a residential drug rehabilitation centre, and Laura was then able to attend the public mortuary and identify her father's body, for which difficult duty the court now thanks you, Laura.

So we have the answer to our first question: the deceased's full name was Robert John Radcliffe, and he was resident at Flat 1, Riverview Gardens, and he was born, according to his birth certificate, on November 12th 1961, in Leeds.

Where did she go. Why did she never go back to the flat when she knew he was waiting. How could she just forget. How could she just let someone else. Was she trying to. Was she making him. We sit and look at his body in the back of the van. We want to ask him but we can't. Did she go back. Did she see him again. Did she climb in through the window one more time and say Dad I'm back but I didn't bring nothing I aint got nothing for you. You'll have to wait for someone else. Is that it. Is that what happened. Did he look up at her and plead with her and say Laura, what the bloody hell is wrong with you I need you to help me. Did she what. Did she look at him for as long as she could bear and say Dad I needed you for a long time didn't I and where were you. What were you doing. You were just sitting here feeling sorry for yourself and drinking yourself to death with your so-called fucking mates. Or did she only wish she had said that. Is she glad now she didn't. Did he say Laura love I aint dead yet. Did he say Laura don't go. Did he say You watch I'll stop drinking right now. I've done it before. If it bothers you that much I'll stop right now. You watch. Did he. Did she climb back out the window while he still said Laura don't go what you doing. Was that the last thing she ever saw ever heard him say. Is that it. Can she get that out of her mind now. Can she ever get that out of her.

CORONER: . . . that his body was discovered in the sitting room of Flat 1, Riverview Gardens, as we shall be hearing from PC Nelson in due course, and that the only door to the flat was bolted from the inside. This might suggest that Mr Radcliffe could only have died in the flat.

However, we'll also hear that the kitchen window, which overlooks the roof of some garages at the side of the flats, was ajar, and that it would have been possible for someone to enter or exit the flat by that route. And in fact we'll hear from Laura that she herself had done just that prior to Mr Radcliffe's death.

So it's possible that someone could have brought Mr Radcliffe's body into the flat, bolted the door from the inside, and left via the kitchen window. However, the evidence from the scene supports the suggestion that Mr Radcliffe came by his death in the location where his body was found: there were no inconsistencies between the pattern of decomposition and the position of the body, for example, and there were no marks or bruises on his clothing or body which suggested he had been dragged or carried anywhere after his death.

Furthermore, as Mr Radcliffe was a very substantially built man, it would have been a significant task to have carried or dragged his body any distance following his death; and any suggestion of his body being moved following death would imply foul play, and no evidence of foul play as a cause of death has been found either during post-mortem examination or in the course of the police investigation.

I therefore find that Robert John Radcliffe did in fact come by his death in the sitting room of Flat 1, Riverview Gardens.

Laura sitting in the court trying to listen. Her skin itching and burning. Her hands squeezed between her thighs because once she starts scratching she knows she won't be able to stop. She should have stayed in the rehab. But there was too much going on. Her dad and everyone else. It was too much to deal with. It weren't the right time. Be a long time before they let her back in now she's signed herself out like that. But maybe they. She's got what mitigating circumstances or something. It'll be a while but she will. She has to. What else can she do. Can't keep on like this for ever. Her bones creaking when she shifts in her chair. Did she think when she started it would be like this. Did we. When we all started. Did she see herself here. Did any of us. Did we think ourselves what like blessed like we might just slip through the net. Or what damned and there weren't no point trying. Was it that. And when her and Danny were lying on the bed together that one time that last time, did she really think she was getting out. Did she think she could sign up for a year in the country and that would be it. She'd be like healed and cleansed and her tears all like wiped away or something more or less like that. That's what Danny meant was it, when he laughed at her like that, like Laura mate it aint that simple. Takes more than fresh air and talking to get clean and stay clean. Lying on the bed together. Did she even know what he wanted from her all that time. Was it what she liked him but she never. Didn't they come close once or twice like a bit of messing around but they never. Was it she wouldn't have minded only it weren't a priority. Was he on her list of things to do once she was clean. Like

227

college, flat, cup of tea in the morning, Danny. Was it like that. Or was Mike right what he thought. Had she been waiting for Mike all this time. Is she still waiting for him now. All that with the clean white sheets and the smell of coffee and the postman whistling and the big empty house and the cars in the drive. Or was that all Danny and his.

CORONER: . . . that the last time she saw her father alive was on the afternoon of the 22nd December, and we will hear from PC Nelson that Mr Radcliffe's body was discovered on the 31st December.

We can conclude therefore that he came by his death during this nine-day period. The Home Office pathologist has stated that death is likely to have occurred between five and nine days before his body was discovered.

This would put the date of his death at somewhere between the 22nd of December, when he was last seen, and the 26th.

This is as accurate as we are able to be, and this is my finding today.

We look at Robert. We listen to the coroner and we look at the policeman and we stand outside the flat waiting for someone to come and kick down the door. And we want to ask. What was it what happened. What was the last thing you saw. Was it Laura climbing back out the window. Or someone else. Was there. Did Mike come back. Did he bring you anything. Did he try and get. Did he start going on about where you kept your money how you owed him a piece of. And now it's payback time pal. Is that what. Did he. Not raising his voice or nothing but. Looking you in the eye. Pulling you up to your feet and. Smacking you one in the face and. Was that what. Always seemed like he might do something. Always on the edge that one but it was all. Did he. Did you even have money to give him we want to ask. All the fury and panic in his voice. And his skinny fists. Someone going Do him now get it over with do him now. Was it that. Was it Mike. All those things he says when he gets on one. I will switch on you. I will take you down. If it comes down to it la I will cut out your heart. Clenching his fists and all fucking trembling. Many have tried and many have failed you know what I'm saying I will outwit you all I will outwit you all. All that. I will keep on la if you push me down I will get up again I will keep on getting up again you watch me pal I will rise I will rise I will. All that. Did he say all. Did he climb in the flat and. Was he talking on the phone taking instructions and. But Mike never done nothing like. He talked but he never. Only grievous bodily harm he ever done was on himself. Knives and needles and cigarettes. Cutting and piercing and burning like. But these things he comes out with. Could have been but. Was it. And what did Robert say. If Mike was stood over him like. Was it.

★ ★ ★

229

CORONER: . . . in answering this question will come from the pathologist's report, to which I shall refer in due course. Before that, though, I would like to go through, firstly, the circumstances surrounding the discovery of Mr Radcliffe's body and, secondly, the circumstances of his life in the days and weeks leading up to his death. I therefore call upon our first witness today to come forward.

COURT USHER: PC Nelson, please.

Place your left hand on the Bible and repeat the words written on the card.

PC NELSON: I do solemnly swear that I shall tell the truth, the whole truth, and nothing but the truth, so help me God.

COURT USHER: Thank you. Please be seated.

CORONER: Thank you. Could you first state your full name and position?

PC NELSON: Thomas Craig Nelson, Police Constable.

CORONER: Thank you. Now, I understand that you were the first officer attending when Mr Radcliffe's body was discovered on the 31st December of last year?

PC NELSON: That is correct, ma'am. There were two of us attending the property, myself and Sergeant Forbes, but as I was the first to locate the body of the deceased I was given the role of first officer attending.

CORONER: Which is a formal role with certain responsibilities.

PC NELSON: That's correct.

CORONER: Now, I have in front of me a copy of the report which is based upon your notes from the scene. Perhaps you could read the relevant section of that to the court? From the beginning until the arrival of the SOC officers?

PC NELSON: Certainly. Sergeant Forbes and myself were requested to attend the property at Flat 1, Riverview Gardens, and if necessary to effect an entrance. This followed a report by a neighbour that the residents had not been seen or heard for a period of approximately one week and that other neighbours had commented on a noticeable smell. Upon arrival at the property we knocked repeatedly at the door, without response. We spoke briefly to the neighbour, who made a number of assertions about the resident and his associates, namely that drugs were used at the property and that noise was a frequent problem. We effected an entry via the front door, and commenced an inspection of the property.

I found the body of Mr Radcliffe lying on the floor of what I took to be the living room, and informed my colleague. A preliminary inspection revealed a significant quantity of blood on the floor, and so we immediately retreated from the premises with the intention of preserving any evidence should it prove to be the scene of a crime. We called for a doctor to certify death and SOC officers to examine the scene. We secured the scene using cordon tape, and –

231

CORONER: Thank you, I think I'll stop you there. So, you entered the flat – you presumably had to break the door open?

PC NELSON: That's correct. The door was locked, and bolted from the inside, but it was in a state of some disrepair so was easily –

All these questions we want to ask. But we can't and. We say nothing. We sit in the van and wait. And the van drives through a gateway and into the backyard of the undertaker's and they open the doors and carry Robert's body away. We go with them. With him. What else can we do. They wash his body. Again. No one ever did that for him when he was alive and now. They bring in a coffin. A plain unvarnished plywood coffin. Nothing special. Nothing with trimmings and linings and a craftsman's attention to. Nothing what no one's been working on for days in the hot dusty sun with the snoring sound of the saw and the plane and the adze going chuck chuck chuck. Nothing like that for Robert now. Must be the biggest coffin they've got though but. With gloved hands they lay him in it. Lay him on the unlined wood. No pillow for his head. No funeral suit to cover his. What is it, shame. Misfortune. No one to pay for a suit he can wear in his. Environmental health paying for this but why would they pay for a suit. No one else. What about Laura. What money has she got anyway. She won't want. Told them she's said her goodbyes and all that and she don't even. And what about Yvonne. Where is she anyway. We look at him in the coffin, his eyes closed and his hands folded awkwardly across his. There are more questions we want to. But we don't. It's too. We can't and they put the lid over him and he's gone. They screw the lid down and the sound of the electric screwdriver is loud in the room like the technician's saw when she cut through his.

CORONER: . . . report of his post-mortem examination, which I do not propose to disclose in its entirety in court today. Rather, I will pick out the most relevant points and then highlight the pathologist's conclusion.

Firstly, toxicology tests on blood samples show no significant levels of alcohol, suggesting that the deceased had not been drinking in the twenty-four to forty-eight hour period prior to his death. The blood tests also found no evidence of cocaine or heroin or other what we might call recreational drugs.

Secondly and conversely, analysis of the liver itself shows extensive cirrhosis, which histological analysis shows to have been caused by alcohol; this indicates that the deceased had in general consumed excessive amounts of alcohol over a prolonged period of time. In the opinion of the pathologist, the blood found on the floor of the flat, and in the kitchen sink, is most likely to have resulted from vomiting caused by the advanced cirrhosis.

Blood was found in the trachea, large airways and lungs, showing that Mr Radcliffe probably aspirated blood and vomit into his lungs prior to death.

Thirdly, examination of the lungs shows destruction of the airspaces, caused by prolonged exposure to cigarette smoke, which would have led to pronounced shortness of breath.

Fourthly, the pathologist found evidence of advanced heart disease, and narrowing of the coronary arteries by approximately seventy to eighty per cent. In simple terms, this means that the arteries supplying blood to the heart had become narrowed by fatty deposits, greatly depriving the heart muscle of oxygen and nutrients, which may have contributed to his death.

Fifthly, the pathologist found no food in Mr Radcliffe's digestive system, suggesting that Mr Radcliffe hadn't eaten anything for a period of approximately twenty-four to forty-eight hours before his death. This would not have been a cause of death – the human body can survive for much longer periods without food – but it's quite possible that he had become weakened as a result.

Sixthly, there was extensive bruising found to Mr Radcliffe's body, and some to his face. In the pathologist's opinion, this bruising is consistent with that caused by falls rather than with acts of violence against him. The pathologist also notes the lack of defence injuries, and notes that there is no evidence of violence or struggle at the scene of death.

The final point made by the pathologist is something of an aside, in that there is no evidence of it being a contributory factor to Mr Radcliffe's death. A fragment of metal was discovered in Mr Radcliffe's skull, just behind his left ear. The pathologist also found what appeared to be an entry wound for this fragment, which was well healed and appeared to be a number of years old. Although the pathologist finds no evidence of this directly contributing to Mr Radcliffe's death, he does note that a previous head injury can be a risk factor in alcohol withdrawal related seizure, which I'll come on to in a moment.

The pathologist concludes that a number of factors may have caused or contributed to Mr Radcliffe's death: chronic lung disease, the coronary artery disease, the bleeding from the gullet entering into the lungs, the lack of food and shortness of breath putting pressure on an already overworked heart. He also notes that Mr Radcliffe appears to have stopped drinking in the days prior to his death, and comments that it is known for long-term alcoholics who abruptly stop drinking to suffer epileptic seizure leading to death as a result. However, there is no way of ascertaining whether this has occurred from a post-mortem examination, and so the pathologist is only able to note the possibility.

This concludes my account of the pathologist's report.

Before using these findings as a basis for the answer to our fourth question in court today, I would like to examine the circumstances around Mr Radcliffe's death a little more closely. I therefore call our second witness this morning.

All these questions. Why did she ever go back and see her dad that first time. What took her back. What was so wrong with living at home. With her mum. With Paul. It was different though things had changed had they. When they first left Robert they lived with her nan for a while. And she liked her nan. She was close to her nan was she. Kept saying how good it was to have them back. Kept saying she'd always known Robert was trouble and they were much better off now. With her. And even when they moved into their own place her nan gave it all I'll always be here for you you know that don't you I'll always be here. And then Paul. What. Stopping around the place more and more and then he was just there. And then her nan didn't come round and they didn't go round there and that was that. Who can you trust. Who can you fucking. And later Paul started going I don't expect you to call me Dad that's entirely up to you but I hope you'll remember who's been here all these years. And if she'd stayed at home. If she'd gone back to. The way all this came out when they were sitting around in their groups at that rehab place. Hadn't thought about any of that for years and then. Had she. If she'd gone back to her mum's. Would she. Was it just that she wanted to know. Was that all. Or did something else. Jesus. Laura sitting in the coroner's court and all the questions they didn't. Like. What did your father mean to you. Why did you ever go back to him then. What was it your mum did or didn't do. And what about Paul. And what took you back to your father's the second time. Once you'd seen him there and you knew. Did you think you could do something. Did you think you could save him. Or were you just desperate by then. After all the. Some kind of defeat or loss or. After those summers full of friends and fields and music and drugs and days and nights stretched out under boundless skies. Thinking nothing could go wrong. Thinking nothing could touch this. And then long winter nights shivering in a van on threatened sites full of mud and tat and travellers with nowhere left to go. Who'd had all the dreaming beaten out of them in that beanfield and given up on hoping for anything more than the next bag. And they called it a battle. First they came for the miners and then they. Could always get good gear but it wasn't. She wanted. So what was it then she went trailing back to her dad. Thinking he'd what like come running out to meet her while she was still down the other end of the street or something. Was that what she. When instead he couldn't hardly remember her name.

★　　★　　★

CORONER: . . . and you were familiar with the other people who spent time there, and with your father's daily routine?

LAURA: Yeah.

CORONER: And am I right in understanding that you actually lived in the flat as a child?

LAURA: Yeah.

CORONER: But you moved away with your mother when you were, how old?

LAURA: Don't know. Seven.

CORONER: And you came back to stay with your father more recently?

LAURA: Yeah.

CORONER: How recently, would you say?

LAURA: About three years.

CORONER: And as far as you're aware, your father has lived in that flat for the whole period, since you were a child right up until the time of his death.

LAURA: Yeah.

CORONER: And do you know why the council housing department are under the impression that they'd evicted your father some years previous to his death?

LAURA: Don't know.

CORONER: Were you aware of any attempt being made to evict him, during the time you were there?

LAURA: No.

CORONER: He didn't talk about it, express any anxiety or concern?

LAURA: No.

CORONER: And you wouldn't say that the level of his drinking had any connection with any potential eviction or financial difficulty?

LAURA: Not really, he'd been drinking like that for years anyhow.

CORONER: Would you describe him as a heavy drinker?

LAURA: Don't know. Depends what you call heavy.

CORONER: Well, could you say how much he drank each day, typically?

LAURA: Depends how much he could get. One or two bottles, I suppose.

CORONER: Of what?

LAURA: Mostly cider.

CORONER: A bottle being how much?

LAURA: Big bottles, three-litre bottles, more if they're on special.

CORONER: Well, I'm not an expert, but I think we can say that between three and six litres of cider a day qualifies as heavy drinking, don't you?

LAURA: (*inaudible*)

CORONER: Well, I'm just trying to build up a picture of his general health at the time of his death. The toxicology report, as you've heard, found a very low level of alcohol in his bloodstream, although from the state of his liver and what you've told us he was quite clearly an alcoholic. Do you know why he hadn't drunk any alcohol prior to his death?

LAURA: No.

CORONER: He hadn't said anything about wanting to stop drinking?

LAURA: No, only (*inaudible*).

CORONER: Only what?

LAURA: Only, I mean, he knew about me going to rehab, he found out about it like. I told him, I mean. He might have thought, after that, you know.

CORONER: He might have decided to do some rehab of his own, you mean?

LAURA: (*inaudible*)

CORONER: Well, that would only be supposition.

Or was it Ben. Climbing in and. What was it. The way he did that pigeon that time it was like he could do any. The way he joined in on Steve when it weren't nothing to do with. Just for the kicks. Something wrong with that one. Something wrong in the head. Something always about to boil over and. Where did he go. When he said he'd take the food up there. What did he do with. If he didn't. And when. Where was Ben. Did he do something. Did he go in looking for money or looking for something else. Just for the kicks. Robert looking at him like he was still a boy like he wouldn't do no harm. Taking the punches like they weren't no matter. Was it. But Ben wouldn't chance it on. Robert was sick but he was still a big. Did he. Watching the boy scramble out through the window and laughing and reaching for another drink but there weren't no drinks there. Or he had one drink left and he kept putting it back. Putting it back in the. Going if Laura can do it so can. I'll show. Who does she think. All high and mighty moral. When she's just a. If she can. And a pain somewhere. And coughing and coughing and finding blood in his hands when he was. And coughing more blood. And going to the kitchen sink and watching the blood spew out. Going Christ what's happening now. The blood on his. And shaking. Fucking. Hands clattering against the bloody sink and just. A pain somewhere. In his shoulder. In his neck. In his chest. Back in the sitting room and just these fucking tremors. Stretching his arms up to give. Reaching for something up above his head. Reaching out his arms going Christ I can't breathe here what's going on. Or not even a chance to say that or say nothing at all. Christ what's going on.

CORONOR: . . . need to speak aloud for the tape, Laura, rather than just shaking your head.
LAURA: No.
CORONER. Did he eat adequately, as far as you're aware?
LAURA: Yeah. He ate loads.
CORONER: Did he cook for himself?
LAURA: No, he got stuff from the garage, sandwiches and crisps and whatever. Or he got takeaway stuff, chips and pizzas, curries, stuff like that. People got it for him.
CORONER: People bought him food?

241

LAURA: Sometimes, or he gave them the money. It was like in return for letting them use the flat.

CORONER: He gave people money to buy him food?

LAURA: Yeah.

CORONER: They didn't steal it, or take advantage somehow?

LAURA: Sometimes. But if they did they never came back.

CORONER: It sounds as though your father had sufficient money for his needs.

LAURA: Yeah. He had a few things going on. (*Interruption to proceedings. Late arrival of member of public.*)

COURT USHER: This is Mr Mike Crossley, ma'am.

CORONER: Thank you. If you could take your place, Mr Crossley. Thank you. Now, if we can continue, Laura. Was your father often alone in the flat?

LAURA: No. Hardly ever. There was always people around. He liked having people around.

CORONER: And who were these people? Was it always the same group of people?

LAURA: (*inaudible*)

CORONER: I'm sorry, could you repeat that?

LAURA: Thing is like, I'm not being funny or nothing but I've already said all this to the police. Haven't you got their report or something? Can't you just like refer to it and that?

CORONER: Well, as I said before, this is a court of public record, and –

LAURA: Yeah, I know but –

CORONER: And we do need to address all these

facts in full before we can conclude the inquest. I'm happy to take a break if you'd like, however.

LAURA: No, it's all right, whatever, carry on.

CORONER: Thank you. So, when did you last see your father?

LAURA: Before Christmas. A few days before Christmas.

CORONER: And this was the occasion on which you entered the flat by climbing up on to the garage roof and in through the kitchen window?

LAURA: Yeah.

CORONER: And why did you need to enter the flat that way?

LAURA: Because he'd bolted the door and couldn't get out or his chair to come and open it, said he was ill or something.

CORONER: Were you concerned about this?

LAURA: Not really. There was always something wrong with him, he was always coughing or puking or falling over of something. Didn't make much odds if he couldn't get out of his chair one day. Seen worse, you get me?

CORONER: And there were four of you on this occasion, the last time you saw your father?

LAURA: Yeah.

CORONER: And the other three were?

LAURA: Don't really matter now does it.

CORONER: I'm aware of the unfortunate circumstances of this inquest, Laura, but I would be very grateful if we could get these details on to the public record.

LAURA: Yeah right, whatever. (*Expletive*) It was me and Danny and Mike and Ben.

CORONER: And by Mike I take it you mean Mr Crossley here?

LAURA: (*inaudible*)

CORONER: I'll note for the tape that you've nodded agreement. And at this point I would like to acknowledge the presence of Mr Mike Crossley in the court today. Ordinarily I would expect to call you as a witness, Mr Crossley, but as you were involved in a road traffic accident on the 27th December, and medical evidence supplied to me asserts that you have no recollection of the weeks prior to your accident, or indeed subsequent to it when you in fact spent five weeks in an induced coma, I see little benefit in asking you to testify. I do however thank you for your presence here today, albeit as a latecomer, and your stated willingness to be of assistance. I appreciate that your physical condition hasn't made it easy for you to attend. Now, Laura, if we could continue.

We see Mike. And he says Eh now pal I'll be off now then. I got some things I need to. I got a bus to. And we turn and. We see Mike still talking on his phone. Striding out into the middle of the road. His long coat swinging around his. Going I knew this kid at school and he. If they wanted to get a little closer to the truth the double the. Let me tell you a secret pal I've got all sorts up in this. Just so long as you. Road traffic accident is one word for it. More like bosh catch that bus in the face you know what I'm saying pal you know what. Step out in the middle of the road and. Couldn't even get that right. When it came down to. Going too slow and caught it at an angle. The look on the driver's face. Woke up all them weeks later giving it all Where am I where am I. Nurses were good but they weren't actually angels you know what I'm. Weren't no closer to heaven than before and weren't no closer to the other place neither. You know what I'm. I've like descended to the. And come back to tell. So what am I meant to do now like. What's the plan now Mikey pal. Got to have a plan. Takes like resourcefulness and. Takes a lot of. He keeps muttering away like this. Over his shoulder. Down Barford Street and through the markets. Over the footbridge and under the underpass and on up the hill towards the playing fields and the flats. Heading back to the flat because where else can he. Going slow. Two crutches and his legs wrapped in bandages. Crying out each time his foot hits the floor. Keeps going though but. Dragging his feet and leaning all his weight on those metal sticks. Keeps turning to look behind him, down near his ankles, like he thinks there's a dog or a pack of hungry dogs coming after. But there's nothing. What was he trying to. Did he think he could get out that. Did he think that was a way of getting away from. Couldn't even get that right and instead he's here now listening to all these questions and. What does he know. How much does he. Talking on the phone. And his long coat swinging around his. And Laura sitting in the court waiting for all the questions to come to an end.

CORONER: . . . four of you entered the flat by the kitchen window, and stayed there, what, the rest of the day?
LAURA: A few hours, I suppose.
CORONER: And what did you do while you were there?
LAURA: Stuff. You know.
CORONER: You took drugs?
LAURA: (*laughter*) No comment like.
CORONER: I appreciate that you don't want to create any problems for yourself, Laura, but it is important that we get a clear picture of what happened that day. It is the last time we know of that anyone saw your father alive. So, let me rephrase the question – were drugs taken in the flat that afternoon?
LAURA: Yeah. Suppose.
CORONER: Which drugs?
LAURA: Smack. Crack.
CORONER: And did your father take any of these drugs?
LAURA: No. He never did. Never wanted to.
CORONER: No, as would appear to be supported by the pathologist's report. But he had no objection to others taking drugs on the premises?
LAURA: No.

CORONER: Now. You've said in your statement to the police that when you left the flat it was because your father had asked you to buy some food and some alcohol for him, is that correct? And food for his dog?

LAURA: Yeah.

CORONER: And he gave you the money for this?

LAURA: Yeah.

CORONER: And you've said that you went to the petrol station on the city side of the ring road to buy food and drink for him, and for the dog, yes?

LAURA: Yeah.

CORONER: All four of you went?

LAURA: No, just me and Mike.

CORONER: And the other two?

LAURA: They went off to score. To buy drugs.

CORONER: So. You and Mike went to buy the food and drink for your father, but according to your statement, you didn't immediately deliver it to him.

LAURA: (*inaudible*)

CORONER: I'll note for the tape that you've shaken your head, and take that as a no. You say you were, and I quote, a bit sidetracked.

LAURA: (*inaudible*)

CORONER: Can you tell me what you mean by a bit sidetracked? Did anyone deliberately impede you from delivering the food and drink you'd purchased?

LAURA: (*inaudible*)

CORONER: Laura?

LAURA: (*expletive*)

CORONER: Laura, would you prefer to take a short break at this stage?

LAURA: (*inaudible*) No. No one deliberately done nothing. I went off and done some gear and forgot about it for a bit. All right?

CORONER: I see.

LAURA: We went off to the garage and bought the stuff, and when we came out Mike just done one, just like scattered up the road. Didn't say nothing and I weren't that bothered anyway. He does that sometimes. He's a bit like unpredictable and that. No offence, Mike. (*Inaudible interjection from the court.*) I headed back up to the flat, but I bumped into Danny, and he'd just scored, and I was just suddenly desperate for a bit so I told Danny he could come and use my room at the hostel if he split his share of the gear with me. I was going to take the food up to the flat after but I forgot.

CORONER: And did you regularly take drugs in the hostel? It's not permitted, is it?

Nothing but questions in that place. In the rehab. Asking questions about way back. About families and. Sitting around in a circle in a room full of books and flipcharts with the breeze blowing through and the beech trees on the long sloping lawn outside. Posters on the wall going all like Today is the first day of the rest of your whatever. Some bloke going Let's talk about your family now shall we. Are you angry about what happened.

Who do you blame do you blame yourself. And what about your mother. How did you feel when her new partner moved in. What was it that made you leave home when you did. All these questions. And sitting there looking at the floor and biting her nails and looking out at the trees and the sloping lawn. Too much to think about. Too much to say. Going How do you think I felt. And the smart bastard going Well, Laura, it's not about me is it now. Didn't say nothing that first time. But thinking it over. A lot of time for thinking it over in there. And another day saying I just wanted to see for myself after everything my mum had told me about him. Saying She lied to me about other stuff so I thought she'd been lying about him and about them and about why we left. And another day going I thought he'd make me feel better about myself or something like. And everyone else in the circle mumbling agreement with her. Like they knew anything about. But that's what it was like. Supportive and that. Patting everyone on the back for going And then he raped me or whatever. When who knew. Looking for answers and that, and the guidance bloke going Mmm I think we've made some real progress today. And Laura going When she said her and Paul were going to emigrate and they already had jobs lined up and they wanted me to go with them I was so angry I couldn't believe it I was so. And someone else in there going What I miss most about the gear what I struggle most with now is I have to think about things I have to remember things. At least before it was all blocked out. I can take the rattles it's just the dealing with stuff I can't deal with. And everyone clapping like that was headline news or something. Like a revelation and. Someone else going It's like when you're on the gear all your emotions and memories are blocked up it's like being constipated in a way and after a while it gets more comfortable like that like you don't even want the shit to come out. And everyone laughing and clapping. And another day Laura going Thing was even though he was in such a state and what my mum had said was true I think I stuck around because at least he was honest and stuff you get me. The others in the circle going Well done, Laura. Looking out at the leaves and the blossom on the trees and the birds on the sloping lawn. A police car coming up the driveway. And then someone asking for her. Someone talking about her dad. And what was he thinking then. Lying on his back with one hand reaching out behind him and the other scrabbling away at the floor. Tell us that. Will you tell us that. Looking up at the ceiling. And did his life. Flash before his eyes and all that or what. What was there to. Sitting in that chair all those. What was he thinking can you tell will you tell.

LAURA: . . . on a reducing script since August or something, it was part of my order, and I was like basically clean and that, I was down to like fifteen mil. I was booked into rehab for the New Year, no one else knew about it apart from my key-worker and them lot. None of the others knew only they knew I'd been on the script.

CORONER: But on this occasion you decided to take some, what, some heroin?

LAURA: Yeah. I just fancied one last go. And Danny had enough to spare.

CORONER: So you went to your room in the hostel, took the drugs, and forgot to deliver the food until, when, the next day?

LAURA: I never took it.

CORONER: You didn't take the heroin?

LAURA: No I mean I never took the food up to him.

CORONER: No, but in your statement you say you remembered about it the next day, and asked someone else to take it to your father's flat for you?

LAURA: Yeah.

CORONER: And who did you ask exactly?

LAURA: Ben. I was scared I was going to lose my rehab place on account of doing the gear again so I was running around looking for my keyworker to get it sorted, and I found Ben hanging around by the hostel waiting for someone, so I gave him the bag of food and asked him to take it up there. He said he was going up there anyway. I thought it'd be all right. And I weren't worried because I thought someone would have been up there by then anyway, I thought like Heather or Jamesie or Maggie or someone would have been up there and sorted him out. There's always people up there usually.

CORONER: But it seems that no one had been there.

LAURA: No.

The men leave and we stand around the silent sealed box. Night passes and the morning. There are eight of them now. Black suits and black shoes and black leather gloves. They slide him into the back of the van. Three of them climbing into the seats in the front and five of them getting into another car and driving out of the courtyard and out through the gates and out along the main road beside the river which leads to the edge of town. We go with them. What else can we. And what about Heather why didn't she come. Why didn't she go to the flat to help. Did she. Was she there. Did she really go knocking on the door. Banging on the door going Robert open up the door. Shouting in the letterbox and pressing her face up against the filthy glass. Was she there. And when she went off looking for the others or. Off for Christmas dinner at the day centre. Did she forget to say anything to anyone. Or did she think. What. Something like sort of fuck him or serve him right. Did she. Don't it matter now. Did it. Where has she. Who. And when we get to the crematorium the men step out of the car and stand around and wait for the previous service to end. The mourners filing out through the wide glass doors into the gardens on the other side of the building and behind them the tall thin chimney begins to smoke. The men slide Robert's coffin from the back of the van and heave him up on to their shoulders. And not even Laura is here. No one is here. The tall thin chimney begins to. And we could be heaving him up on to our own shoulders but we're too late for that now. We could be throwing flowers and blowing trumpets and singing low mournful songs as he is carried in through the doors of the chapel on the broad black-suited shoulders of men who barely know his name. But we're not and no one is and no one will and it's too late for any of that now. And not even Laura is here. Not even Yvonne is here. But she's miles away now. They carry him up the aisle to the front of the chapel. And with a count of three they drop him from their shoulders and lower him on to a conveyor belt in front of a pair of red curtains and they turn to leave. We stand in a huddle at the back by the. What else can we. The vicar stands at the front in his robes. Holding the service book open and watching the men walking away and when they get to the door he calls them back. He says Am I missing something. They look at him. He says Can you see anyone else. They look down at their. He says I'm not going to stand here and see this man off by myself. He says Is there somewhere more important you. And they turn and walk back up the aisle and take their seats. And the vicar begins. We are gathered here today. All these people going out of their way to treat him right now. After he's. When before they never even.

CORONER: . . . seems that neither Ben nor anyone else delivered the food.

LAURA: No. I don't know. I don't know what happened after that.

CORONER: No, indeed. The police have been unable to track down anyone who did see your father after the time you left the flat, and the neighbour who called them to the premises was unable to recall hearing any visitors after the date she says she saw you and your friends climbing in through the kitchen window. And following your statement to the police, the photographic records of the scene were reviewed and no evidence of the items you described purchasing at the garage could be found. So we must conclude, as we are sadly unable to ask Ben in person, that for whatever reason he didn't or wasn't able to deliver the food.

LAURA: (*inaudible*) (*expletive*)

CORONER: I think we'll leave that line of questioning there; it's unlikely to shed any more light on the cause of your father's death and I can see it is causing you some distress, for which I can only apologies.

Are you happy for us to continue, or would you prefer to take a break?

LAURA: (*inaudible*)

CORONER: Thank you. I have no further questions. If you'd like to return to your seat I shall attempt to conclude our examination of the fourth question I referred to in my introduction.

LAURA: (*inaudible*)

CORONER: Did you have anything further you wanted to add?

LAURA (*inaudible*)

CORONER: No. Right then. Thank you. I'll move on.

Quite simply, we do not and cannot know exactly why Mr Radcliffe died. We can say that there is no evidence of anyone else having been involved, and so no evidence of a criminal act being responsible for his death. We can say that he was in a state of very poor health as a result of his lifestyle, diet and alcoholism. We can say that the condition of his liver, heart and lungs could all have contributed to his death. And we can note the pathologist's remark that a sudden cessation of drinking by long-term alcoholics has been known to result in epileptic seizure, although we cannot say whether this is what happened to Mr Radcliffe.

We might be tempted to speculate as to the reasons why Mr Radcliffe abruptly stopped drinking, and what effects this may have had on his body. We might want to speculate as to why, when the food and drink he was expecting to be brought to him didn't arrive, he failed to venture out and fetch some for himself. We might even want to speculate as to just how he came to be living in quite the degree of self-neglect and squalor he did, and why those around him felt this to be acceptable.

But none of this speculation would be relevant, or admissible, and none of it would help us reach a verdict today, or indeed give us any clearer a picture of the last moments of Mr Radcliffe's life. Ultimately, the exact mechanics and circumstances of his death will remain a mystery to us. And sadly this is often the—

And so did his life flash before his. Did he lie there looking up at the cracked and ruined ceiling thinking over. Or not even thinking just seeing. From the beginning. A child in his mother's. First memories of food and love and fights and shouting and playing and slamming doors. First thoughts of what of leaving home of finding someone to. Walking through the city in the middle of the night with a headful of drink and talk and the miles jolting by beneath his feet and the lights sliding. Finding Yvonne waiting for him outside the pub and what she. Later that night and again the next. Lining up outside the job centre and ending up in the army office. Training and marching and fighting and sleeping in a room with a dozen others. Crawling in the mud. Stripping engines and guns and new recruits. Weeks at sea heading south. The bullets the bombs the one explosion next to his head and the hours stretched out in the long wet grass while the troopships burnt brightly in the grey unsheltered bay. These things whirling through him as what not memories but as moments lived whirling through him while he lay there on the floor. Is that what happened. And did he remember or see or live again all the times with Yvonne. When he came back from the real crisis and they moved into the flat and he found a job and they decorated the flat together and made it theirs. When Laura was born and he lost his job and he kept drinking and drinking until they left. And the pain in his fucking head. And the sound of the softly closing door. And the way she shouted at him and her voice seemed so far away. The way she would stub out her cigarette and push him on to his back for another go and the way she kept going on at him to find another job and he said What can I do there's nothing going what can I do and this pain in my fucking head. And some days that feeling. Like a snared animal flailing around and making it worse. If he kept moving he could bear it but he couldn't get out. And the thing that undone him. When she said I don't understand you, Robert, and I'm never going to this isn't what I wanted this isn't what I want no more. Speaking quietly for once while he just sat there trying not to. This one moment whirling through his head the most as he lay there looking at the ceiling plaster crumble and fall. Was it that. Is that what happened. Did he see or remember or live all these things again. Like a lifetime in a moment. Like a dream of hours poured into. Is that what happens. Is that what happens to us all. When we. Did he see Penny waiting for him to wake. Did he see Danny climb in through the window. Did he see the police creep into the room and light him up. Taking pictures and measurements and putting bags over his head and his hands. Did he see us standing there watching and everything that happened to us before we arrived. Did he see us sitting here now. Is it this. Is this what happens. In the last moment. Is this what's happening to us now. Is this what all this is. Like We are gathered here today.

Is this what all we are seeing now. What Steve sees as he lies on the mattress in his whitewashed room. Ant lying beside him, stiffening and slackening and falling quiet, H waiting for them both to wake, Danny standing in the yard and calling up and throwing stones through the window, that woman Marianne or Marie and the smoke rising from the village and the policeman saying Even the dogs. And the way he fell from the Land Rover while it raced along the track outside Stanley, thinking What kind of war wound is this when the fighting had all been done before he even got off the ship, the fight with Robert and the fights after dark at school and watching the police creep down the hall to where Robert lay and Ant going Look I'll show you what the fuss is all about. And is this what Ben sees as he crouches behind the bins in the carpark basement, the three days rattling in the cells, the way he'd taken Jamesie

258

down in the day centre and the way Mike had disappeared before the police arrived, and himself white-eyed and blue-lipped going over. And Robert being carried out to the van. And his sister slapping him round the face going What did you ever do, and that bloke who paid to take him home and tried to, all that, and Mike giving him that warning, all that It's for your own protection la but you'll need to ease off with that mouth of yours else something might, and what Heather did, so what, and is this what Danny sees, curled up on the phonebox floor, the daylong march around town with no one around and Einstein chasing along at his feet, and slamming the door on Laura's room, and climbing out of the flat with her, and his brother pushing him back out the door and his brother holding him up one time when he was sick all over his bathroom floor, his brother holding him tight, and Robert on the floor, and Robert in the bodybag, and Robert with his chest cut open on the table, and Laura sitting straight-backed in the court with her hands wedged between her thighs, and is this what Heather sees, kneeling beside her bed with the long white curtains blowing into the room and her heart slowed to a stop and the blood all sinking down towards the floor, Danny buzzing away on the intercom and shouting up at the window, her front door crashing in when they came for her kids, the time up on stage when the band let her play, the crowd, the way the crowd looked at her, Jimmy saying Best not tell anyone I'm stopping here though, the judge saying But while you allow your partner to remain in the house, and all those years on the road, and waking up with that tattoo, and Robert being carried in through the chapel door, and the four of them it took to hold her back against the wall, and everything she did to get rid of that and she still sees it all roaring through her now, and is this what Mike sees, all of this, every last moment, as he strides out into the road with his phone pressed against his ear, going No you listen to me pal you listen to me what have you done, what have you gone and done this time, I've been looking everywhere and I can't find no one now they've all gone, what's happened, what have you gone and done, and what about Laura, what about that girl, what have you done to her now, well youse can all stop talking now I feel much better now thank you now I got a bus to catch. And is all this what he sees as he lies there in the hospital bed. Wires and tubes coming out of his body and his shattered bones twisting back. Like healing. And his eyes closed for weeks and some machine going beep and ping and keeping him comatose so his body can. While these visions go surging through his blood. All this. Is it. Is that what all this.

And the red curtains part and the coffin rolls away. There's no music. Who would choose the. The vicar closes his book and thanks the men and they stand and walk away. We follow Robert's coffin. What else can we. On the other side of the curtains. We see two technicians. Opening a heavy steel hatch and rolling the coffin through. Sealing it shut. Turning dials and pressing buttons and standing aside to let us watch through a thick glass panel as the flames begin to rise. Blue and orange jets of fire in long straight rows. Like an oven. Tongues of fire. And the thin wood of the coffin quickly chars and smoulders and crumbles into ash around his body, and his flesh spits and cooks in the roaring furnace heat, melting around his bones which splinter and crack in the blinding firelight. Outside the tall thin chimney. Footsteps and voices and organ music in the chapel as the next group of. Minutes pass. Little more. What's left of him. The burning. Charred pieces of bone and. The technicians open the door and rake over the embers and fire up the furnace again. The blue flames burn cleanly now. They rake the ashes through a grille and into a steel pan to cool. They set them aside. What's left of him. And what do we do now.

We sit at the back of the court. And we watch Mike. Struggling to his feet. His crutches crashing against the chairs in front as he hauls himself to his. The court usher saying If you could just. Laura with a hand over. And Mike going I've had enough of this pal I'm. I'll see you around I'll. Dragging his feet across the. And everyone. And crying out each time his foot. The door closing behind him and the room still ringing with his presence and we watch Laura. The tilt of her head as she watches the coroner gather her. And she realises there are no more. But what about. Everything else she needs to know. Everything else she wants. But she won't. It's not. It's what is it outside the remit of the court. Isn't it always. Aren't we always outside the remit. We watch. Pushing her hair back behind her. Rubbing her hands on her. Where will she go now. What will she. Leave town and. Stick to her script and wait for another place in. Will they let her have another. And that keyworker what can he. Will she get up again. What else can she. Will she keep getting up again. And will she wake up in the morning and think about making a cup of tea. Putting on the kettle and waiting for it to boil. Finding a mug and a teabag and. Is there space in her head for. Watching the teabag rise to the surface and turn and fall. Can she give herself the time. Is she halfway there and. Waiting for the tea to brew. Scooping out the bag and dropping it in the bin and stirring in the milk. Can she make plans now. Is there space in her head for. Sitting at the table with the steam rising out of the mug and catching the light and turning in the air.

And Mike still struggling down the street. His two crutches scraping along the ground. And crying out. Huh hah huh. A crowd of pigeons scattering at the sound of his voice and circling overhead. Settling on a rooftop and rising and circling and settling again and Mike going. Huh. Hah. Huh.

The coroner signs something and stamps some documents with an inky thud. And stands up and. Smiles at Laura one more time and glances at the. And the policeman already getting to his feet as she steps down from the bench with the file of papers under her arm and the usher says All rise will the court please.

We rise. What else can we do, we fucking rise.